James White

The seasons and miscellaneous poems

James White

The seasons and miscellaneous poems

ISBN/EAN: 9783337207007

Printed in Europe, USA, Canada, Australia, Japan

Cover: Foto ©Andreas Hilbeck / pixelio.de

More available books at **www.hansebooks.com**

THE SEASONS

AND

MISCELLANEOUS POEMS,

BY

THE REV. JAMES WHITE,

(Vicar of Oakengates, Shropshire,)

AND AUTHOR OF "THE SABBATH SCHOOL RECITANA."

SECOND EDITION, REVISED AND ENLARGED.

"These, as they change, *Almighty Father*, these
Are but the varied God ; the rolling year
Is full of Thee."—*Thomson.*

LONDON :
SIMPKIN, MARSHALL & Co.

WELLINGTON, SALOP :
HOBSON & Co., SHROPSHIRE PRINTING WORKS.
1886.

PREFACE.

—:o:—

THE Author cannot be supposed to have penned his "Seasons" on the summit of *Olympus*, where wind, rain, and clouds, are said to be unknown. He has, to the best of his ability, described the leading features of the "Seasons," and trusts that his lucubrations will meet with some kindly attention.

He does not presume to have emulated the graphic delineations and classic style of a THOMSON; but entertains a hope, that his sentiments will prove generally correct, and be acceptable to his readers.

To interest the young, and lead such to habits of reading and thinking; and to cultivate a love of Nature, with the hope that they may be "led from Nature up to Nature's God," is the chief desire of the Author; and if this little volume should in any degree accomplish this end, he will be amply rewarded.

PREFACE TO THE SECOND EDITION.

——.o:——

The first edition of this Volume appeared in 1873, and was soon out of print. Since then, another edition has been so repeatedly asked for, that the Author again commits it to the press, with the addition of more than twenty new poems. It is hoped that its acceptability will again be fully demonstrated by a rapid sale.

Contents.

—:o:—

THE SEASONS.

—:o:—

MISCELLANEOUS POEMS.

National.

Local.

Religious.

Family Reminiscences.

Various.

Valedictory.

—:o:—

———:o:———

THE SEASONS.

———:o:———

Spring.

DULL Winter's past—bright Spring is here,
With balmy smiles our hearts to cheer,
  Strewing our path with flowers ;
The hills and dales with verdure teem,
And sweetly flows the purling stream
  Through fields and garden bowers.

Each day increases now in length,
And Sol's bright beams augment in strength,
  The atmosphere how warm !
The florist plies his spade and hoe,
The plants he watches while they grow,
  And shields them from all harm.

See, from their lowly grassy beds,
Spring flowers are lifting up their heads,
  And num'rous charms unfold ;
Cowslips and daisies fresh are seen,
With countless buttercups between,—
  As if bedecked with gold.

The snowdrop, earliest child of Spring,
Has pass'd away—sweet, fragile thing,
  So delicately white ;
The crocus too, of early birth,
Just peered above its bed of earth,
  Then disappeared from sight.

Fruit trees are clad in newest dress,—
Green leaves and blossoms gay possess,
　　How exquisitely grand !
The hawthorns too our notice claim,
And shrubs of varied size and name,
　　All beautify the land.

Now zephyrs kiss the flow'rets fair,
Scattering perfume everywhere,
　　And fanning wood and brake ;
Sweet sounds come floating on the breeze,
And there's a rustling 'mong the trees,
　　A ripple on the lake.

Upon yon verdant, sunny bank,
Where buttercups and daisies rank,
　　Are shedding fragrance round,
A troop of lambs are seen at play,
Running and leaping all the day,
　　From hedge to hedge they bound.

The grass,—exub'rant, fresh, and new,
Bestrewed with flowers of every hue,
　　Adorns each field and glade ;
The hedges are with foliage dress'd,
And all things seem with beauty blest,
　　In sunshine and in shade.

In yonder fields the shooting grain,
Which had for months in darkness lain,
　　Is peering 'bove the earth ;
The clouds their gentle showers distil,
And these with solar influence will
　　To Summer fruits give birth.

Where'er we turn our eyes we see
In earth and sky, in flower and tree,
   Almighty power display'd ;
Yon blue expanse with glory tinged,
This sylvan grove with blossoms fringed,
   Were by His wisdom made.

The forest trees are verdant now,
For leaves adorn each twig and bough,
   And flutter in the breeze ;
The feathered tribes enjoy the change,
They through the forest gladly range,
   And sing among the trees.

Children are strolling through the wood,
Sweet emblems of the rising bud,
   How happy is their mien !
And others in their childish glee,
Are sporting 'neath the wide-spread tree
   Upon the village green.

See, in that neighb'ring well-ploughed mead,
A sower's casting forth the seed,
   He steps with measured tread ;
Behind a flock of hungry Crows,
Are picking up the seed he sows,
   Like thieves with signs of dread.

A harrow follows in the rear,
And hence the Crows are full of fear
   Lest harm should them befall ;
They light, then rise, and light again,
And thus they steal, and steal the grain,
   Mischievous one and all.

A husbandman is whistling near,
The joys of Spring his spirits cheer,
   He seems from trouble free ;
And while he clips the hedge with care,
He breathes the pure, salubr'ous air,
   How blest with health is he !

But hark ! I hear a well-known bird,
Its mellow tone is plainly heard,
   Monotonous 'tis true ;
It is the Cuckoo's voice I hear,
Reminding us that Spring is here,
   When earth her charms renew.

The Swallow, too, is here again,
And other birds that cross'd the main
   To seek a warmer shore ; .
O how they twitter, chirp, and scream,
How full of life and joy they seem,
   That they're returned once more !

The Swallows fly with open bill,
And multitudes of insects kill,
   Throughout their rapid flight ;
They skim the surface of the lake,
And oft discordant music make,
   With seeming great delight,

The birds their nests are building now,
Some choose a high extended bough,
   And some a humbler seat ;
One goes and brings what he thinks best,
The other sits and forms the nest,
   And makes it warm and neat.

Their various motions while they build,
Both pleasure and instruction yield,
   As to and fro they roam ;
How quick they move,—no time they lose,
In bringing hay, moss,—what they choose,
   To form each humble home.

The Crow selects a lofty tree,
The Lark, the verdant flowery lea,
   On which to place the nest ;
And high upon the old church tower
The Swallow builds,—the garden bower
   The Goldfinch thinks the best.

And where the gushing river flows,
And on its bank the gorse-bush grows,
   The Wren constructs her seat ;
A nest most curious to behold,
Made quite secure against the cold,
   A safe and snug retreat.

The Cuckoo—strangest bird of all,
Ne'er builds in bush, or tree, or wall,
   Nor on the grassy plot ;
She ventures in another's nest,
And for a moment takes a rest,
   Then quits the dang'rous spot.

A pretty Goldfinch's warbling near,
His canzonet I love to hear,
   And view his dappled coat ;
O what a lively little fellow,
His cadence rich and truly mellow,
   But very brief his note.

The Lark ascends on gladsome wing,
And as he mounts we hear him sing,
　And watch his airy flight ;
The Linnet too, throughout the day,
Warbles a most enchanting lay,
　With signs of great delight.

A host of songsters fill the air
With strains which nought can e'er compare,
　Heaven's songs alone excel ;
The sweetest note comes from yon bush,
Where sits the mottle-breasted Thrush,
　He sings both loud and well.

Amid the varied pleasing sounds,
With which the atmosphere abounds,
　And thoughtful minds elate ;
I hear the Stock-dove's plaintive note,
The cadence comes from woods remote,
　He mourns an absent mate.

The farm-yard now is all alive,
The bees are buzzing round the hive,
　And visit flow'rets gay ;
As soon as morn begins to break,
Discordant sounds the poultry make,
　Which last throughout the day.

The quacking tribe have sought the pool,
And float upon its surface cool,
　Or bask upon its brim ;
The water sparkles in the light,
Its visitors show great delight,
　And plumage neatly trim.

The faithful hen, with num'rous brood,
Is searching for their daily food,
　　And scratches everywhere ;
Anon she calls them 'neath her wings,
And screens from harm the helpless things,
　　They've sure protection there.

The great variety of sounds,
The charms with which the earth abounds,
　　And Sol's resplendent glow,
With gratitude our hearts should fill,
To HIM above, whose sov'reign will
　　Makes life through nature flow.

Of childhood's bloom and youthful growth,
When faculties are budding forth,
　　This season is a type ;
The rising plant and opening flower,
Are emblems of youth's growing power,
　　Before 'tis fully ripe.

O were this season always ours,
Its sunny smiles and golden hours,
　　Designed for constant use !
But Summer's heat and Autumn's fall,
And Winter's cold,—great changes all,
　　Will everywhere produce.

Thy charms, bright Spring, vast and sublime,
Pourtray the beauties of yon clime,
　　Unchanged by cold or heat,
Where flow'rets bloom and never die,
And things enduring greet the eye,
　　All lovely and complete.

" Still waters " too, and " pastures green,"
And dazzling rays of heavenly sheen,
    An Eden sure is this !
Angelic hosts their voices raise,
In hymning their Creator's praise,
    And nought can mar their bliss.

To that blest land the Christian tends,
Assured that when his journey ends
    On earth, he'll there reside ;
And never more by storms be toss'd,
When he cold Jordan's stream has cross'd,
    He'll evermore abide.

A Morning in Spring.

'Tis morning, and the " King of Day,"
Maintains his wide triumphant sway,
    How potent are his rays !
The atmosphere is vocal now,
For feathered choirs from twig and bough,
    Pour forth their matin lays.

The sprightly Lark is warbling high,
Beyond the stretch of human eye,
    But quite distinctly heard ;
Let sluggish man a lesson learn
To offer praise at early morn,
    From this most charming bird.

The landscape smiles, and teems with life,
All things are now with gladness rife,
    And hail Aurora's reign ;
The flow'rets lift their gorgeous heads,
Sweet scent abounds where Flora treads
    O'er valley, hill, and plain.

With books in hand, a sprightly boy,
A picture true of health and joy,
    Is hastening to the school ;
He whistles loud,—then hums awhile,
His face is radiant with a smile,
    He shames the dunce and fool.

And there I see a butterfly
With wings of almost every dye,
    Fluttering in the air ;
An insect wonderful is this,
'Merged from a state of chrysalis,
    Quite beautiful and fair.

But ah ! a cruel boy has caught
That pretty fly,—and now its coat
    Of many hues is torn :
E'en such is life,—now all is gay,
But earthly joys soon pass away,
    And leave us sad and lorn.

There goes a brawny son of toil,
With spade in hand to till the soil,
    Smoking his Indian weed ;
How pleasant is his rural life,
From town and city's din and strife,
    He happily is freed.

The morning breeze I love to share,
And stroll through fields and meadows where
    The flowers rich fragrance shed ;
I love to gaze on Nature's face,
For there the hand divine I trace,
    And to adore I'm led.

This spreading shrub,—that op'ning bud,
Yon oak which tempests has withstood,
    Also each tender blade ;
These fragrant flowers,—that shooting grain,
The solar heat,—the fruitful rain,
    Were by th' Almighty' made.

An Evening in Spring.

How cool to walk in evening's shade,
Along the verdant, flowery glade,
    And view its mottled vest ;
When dew is lying all around,
And vapour overspreads the ground,
    And Sol has sunk to rest.

What stillness ! scarce one sound is heard,
The wind is hush'd, and mute each bird,
    The flocks quite silent are ;
The flow'rets droop beneath the dew,
And in yon sky of deepest blue,
    I see the evening star.

As night draws on, unnumbered stars,
With Saturn, Jupiter, and Mars,
    Will deck the vast expanse ;
And as they one by one appear,
Both large and small—some dim, some clear,
    The scene will much enhance.

The crescent moon appears in view,
How small her disc—how pale her hue,
    But welcome is her light ;
Her silvery face I love to see,
She sheds her beams o'er land and sea,
    And radiates the night.

And as I gaze at yon blue sky,
Majestic clouds are floating by,
    Anon they hide the moon ;
Their shadows fall upon the ground,
And quickly darken all around,
    But disappear as soon.

A rippling brook flows near my feet,
Its mystic music wild and sweet,
    Falls gently on the ear ;
Its water pure, reflects the light,
In it I see the " Queen of Night,"
    'Tis mirrored true and clear.

Flow on, flow on, thy limpid streams
In lunar rays and solar beams,
    Sparkle like diamonds bright ;
Thy sloping banks, they gently lave,
Where scented flow'rets sweetly wave,
    And greet our wond'ring sight.

Soon night her curtain will withdraw,
And Sol display his peerless glow,
　　Enlivening all around ;
The dew dry up—the vapour chase—
Eclipse each planet's radiant face,
　　And make earth's joys abound.

This calm retreat--this verdant glade,
Yon crescent moon, and evening's shade,
　　That laughing rill as well ;
The clouds which float—the stars which glow,
All, all, their Maker's impress show,
　　And of HIS goodness tell.

Summer.

───

BEAUTEOUS Spring has sped away,
With all its youthful charms so gay,
　　And Summer bright is here ;
Rendering earth enamelled ground,
And redolent with fragrance round ;
　　How lovely things appear !

The trees in ample foliage dress'd,
The shrubs with num'rous charms possess'd,
　　And diff'rent shades of green ;
The verdure which adorns yon hill,
The smiling fields, and laughing rill,
　　Enhance the pleasing scene.

All nature teems with signs of life—
Earth, air, and water, all are rife
 With sights we love to see ;
The orb of day pours forth his rays,
The feather'd tribe, mellifl'ous lays,
 From every shrub and tree.

This sylvan grove,—yon golden bowers,
Display unnubered fruits and flowers
 Of various shapes and hues ;
Luxuriant moss, plants, shrubs, and trees,
Spread richest fragrance on the breeze,
 And thoughts divine infuse.

The garden's variegated beds
Where flow'rets lift their gorgeous heads,
 And all their tints display,
Afford the thoughtful mind a treat,
Regale the sense with odour sweet,
 And man his toil repay.

These sunflowers beautiful and tall,
These honeysuckles 'gainst the wall,
 And pansies rich and gay ;
All fragrant, bright, and fair in June,
But ah ! how frail—short liv'd—how soon
 They droop, and pass away !

The humming bee and butterfly
In quest of food are hieing by,
 They visit shrub and flower ;
And there the little prudent ant
Is laying by what she may want,
 Improving every hour.

The ant and bee a lesson give,
To teach man how he ought to live,
   And all his powers engage
In gathering up an ample store,
Of needful good and useful lore,
   Against the chill of age.

A merry group are making hay,
And thus they pass the live-long day,
   None idle,—all are throng ;
Anon loud laughter greets the ear,
For jokes are pass'd, and speeches queer
   Are made by old and young.

Each face with perspiration streams,
For Sol darts down his potent beams
   As if to rout them quite ;
But each with vigour plies the rake,
And thus unite the hay to make,
   While all is warm and bright.

The cows o'ercome by solar heat
Have sought a shaded cool retreat
   Beneath th' umbrageous trees :
And there a young unbroken steed
Is prancing round the spacious mead,
   And sniffs the gentle breeze.

A botanist, for plants quite rare,
Is searching now with anxious care
   In Nature's ample book ;
He strolls along the sparkling rill
And down the glen, and o'er the hill,
   He pries in every nook.

Perchance a valued plant he spies,
(To him a priceless, peerless prize),
　　And roots it from the spot ;
His bosom heaves with purest pleasure,
As off he hastens with his treasure,
　　To plant it near his cot.

See, in that pond the fishes rise,
(Diversified in name and size),
　　And all their powers employ ;
Myriads of insects dance and play
Throughout the lengthened Summer day,
　　All full of life and joy.

The angler stands with baited hook,
Beside the river, lake, and brook,
　　To catch the finny tribe ;
He casts it forth with steady hand,
And soon he brings the fish to land
　　Which take the tempting bribe.

Now invalids in search of health,
And men of pleasure, fashion, wealth,
　　To various climes repair ;
The railway trains vast numbers take,
And boats on ocean, river, lake,
　　Immortal cargoes bear.

Sea-bathers seek the ocean's side,
And gladly plunge beneath the tide
　　To strengthen nerve and limb ;
But some for pleasure venture there,
And quite enjoy a treat so rare,
　　As to and fro they swim.

I love to watch the ocean's wave
Yon rugged rocks pacific lave,
   And spread along the strand ;
Unnumbered vessels gaily ride
Upon the ocean deep and wide,
   And pass from land to land.

The schoolboys now have time to play,
For Summer's brought its holiday,
   The satchel's quite forgot ;
They stroll about from morn till night,
In rural sports take great delight,
   How happy is their lot !

There goes a boy with stealthy tread,
To parent-birds a perfect dread—
   Nest-robbing is his pleasure ;
He skulks along the hedge's side,
And then across the ditch he'll stride
   To grasp their precious treasure.

Some children hate such cruel sport,
And when to fields and woods resort
   It is to gather flowers ;
Or else to join in some nice play,
And thus they blithely wile away
   Bright childhood's happy hours.

From yonder mount the prospect's clear,
And sounds melodious greet the ear—
   Above, below, around ;
The bleating flock,—the lowing herd,—
The snorting steed,—the warbling bird,
   Make hills and dales resound.

A sketcher, or a rural bard,
Is seated on the grassy sward
   Of yonder eminence ;
He's pencilling the landscape fair,
Which stretches round him everywhere,
   And seen quite well from thence.

High cloud-capt mountains bound the view,
O'er them a beaut'ous sky of blue,
   As far as eye can stretch ;
Below, there's water, wood, and rocks,
With grazing herds and snow-white flocks,—
   A splendid scene to sketch.

And there, a noble cascade's streams
In solar light with brightness gleams,
   Quite deaf'ning is its roar ;
The cliffs o'er which its waters leap,
Are bold, majestic, towering, steep,
   Where eagles only soar.

Summer, thy beauties countless are,
In real worth transcending far
   Earth's gems and polished gold ;
Poets may sing, and limners paint,
Their best description is but faint,
   Thy charms can ne'er be told !

But Summer time will glide away,
Its sunshine and its flow'rets gay,
   All, all will soon be past ;
And all our sublunary bliss,
However pure its nature is,
   Will but a short time last.

And is their nought in Summer time,
To damp our bliss?   Is this fair clime
  Like Paradise of old?
O no, the heat, the rain, the dust,—
Oppress, besmear, and damp, and rust,
  And dim the finest gold.

Then let our contemplations turn
From earth to heaven,—and daily learn
  The way to yon bright place,
Where all is peace, and love, and joy,
And souls redeemed their tongues employ
  To praise the Saviour's grace.

What endless glory gilds each brow!
Their beauty is unfading now,
  Such bliss can not be told :
Amaranthine flowers deck the plains,
And angels chant immortal strains,
  And strike their harps of gold.

There, heat and cold's alike unknown,
And Jesus dwells amidst His own,
  By shining hosts adored ;
" Eye hath not seen, ear hath not heard,"
What HE in wisdom hath prepared
  For those who love the Lord.

A Morning in Summer.

Soon ebon Nox withdraws her face,
And lov'd Aurora takes her place,
  More brightly every hour ;
When *Phœbus* first appears in view
Cancer assumes a blushing hue,
  And all things feel his power.

He paints the clouds that roll on high,
The mist from off the mountains fly
  Before his glorious blaze ;
His potent heat dries up the dew,
And vegetation smiles anew
  Beneath his cheering rays.

The Lark, while dew hangs on his breast,
Awakes, and quickly leaves his nest,
  To gain his 'customed height ;
His wings now flutter—then they float,
And all the while he tunes his throat,
  Till lost to mortal sight.

A thousand warblers soon awake,
In bush, and tree, and thorny brake,
  And plume each breast and wing ;
Then each bird pours a cheering lay,
Sweetly caroling all the day,
  They make the welkin ring.

And now struts forth bold Chanticleer,
And calls his mates in accents clear
   To leave their several seats ;
His family and neighbours all,
Obey his oft-repeated call,
   And quit their snug retreats.

The husbandman resumes his toil,
With strength renewed he tills the soil,
   And sings a lively air ;
A shepherd seated on yon rock,
Is looking o'er his bleating flock,
   To see if all are there.

A happy swain, with horse and cart,
Is hast'ning to the nearest mart,
   To sell his master's corn ;
He whistles loud, with spirits gay,
He cracks his whip, and plods his way,
   As cheerful as the morn.

A milk-maid with her stool and pail,
Is tripping lightly down the vale
   To yonder dasied field ;
The patient kine her coming wait,
And soon they will, close by the gate,
   The precious fluid yield.

With mellow voice she hums a tune,
Her cheeks are like the rose in June,
   Her eyes like diamonds bright ;
The cattle love to hear her song,
Will toss their heads, and round her throng,
   As if enraptured quite.

Zephyrs are sweeping o'er the ground,
And scatter rich perfume around,
　　Moving each plant and flower ;
The breeze now gently waves the corn,
And breathes soft whispers through the thorn.
　　Which forms the garden bower.

What pleasing sights ! what joyous sounds !
What animation now abounds
　　O'er every vale and hill !
The birds proclaim their Maker's praise,
And through Creation vast I trace
　　Almighty power and skill.

An Evening in Summer.

'TIS sweet to walk at eventide,
Through fields and by the river's side,
　　And o'er the grassy mound,
Where Sol his parting lustre sheds,
Where flow'rets droop their lovely heads,
　　And dew-drops sparkle round.

I love to view the setting sun,
When he the western goal has won,
　　And sheds his crimson light ;
Giving the ocean, clouds, and sky,
A rich and variegated dye
　　As he departs from sight.

Now sable night has closed around,
And there I see upon the ground
   The glow-worm's mystic light—
A little, wondrous, brilliant spark,
Shining pleasantly in the dark
   Throughout the Summer night.

Hush ! lightly tread, all nature's still,
Save the flowing, murmuring rill,
   And river's constant gush ;
For Philomela pours her lay,
She sings by night as well as day,
   Sequestered in the bush.

Nocturnal songster of the grove,
Near thy retreat I love to rove,
   To hear thy peerless song ;
Such varied strains,—all rich and sweet,
With music's num'rous charms replete,
   To thee alone belong.

But lo ! a Bat is flitting by
And now I hear a doleful cry
   From yon old ivied-wall ;
It is the Screech-Owl's piercing scream,
To break night's stillness it would seem,
   And to alarm us all.

And now upon the breeze is borne,
A sound from yonder field of corn,
   As strange as aught can make ;
It is the Landrail's monotone,
Perchance he finds himself alone,
   And hence his constant crake.

The stars are twinkling o'er my head,
And here and there a strip of red
   Adorns the azure sky ;
The silvery moon now hides her face,
But shortly will resume her place,
   And rule and shine on high.

Ye " floating fountains "—beaut'ous all,
I love to gaze as on ye roll
   In majesty profound ;
But soon ye will dissolve in rain,
And thus return to earth again,
   To fertilize the ground.

How fitting now in evening's shade,
While wand'ring through this green arcade,
   Where feathered tribes repose,
To contemplate that glorious ONE,
Who made the ocean, earth, and sun,
   And every plant that grows !

Each little bird—each painted flower,
Displays His wondrous skill and power,
   Likewise yon stars that shine,—
All, all were by His wisdom plann'd,
And man himself proclaims the hand
   That made him is divine.

A Sabbath Morning in Summer.

ANOTHER week of toil has fled,
Its hours and days have quickly sped,
　　And Sabbath morn is here :
O blessed day ! the best of seven,
Sweet emblem of yon rest in heaven,
　　To every Christian dear.

What sacred stillness reigns around !
The earth itself seems hallowed ground,
　　And Sol appears to smile ;
Serenely fair is yon blue sky,
The cheerful Lark is soaring high,
　　And warbling all the while.

Canorous sounds now fill the air,
For birds are singing everywhere,
　　On shrub, and tree, and wall ;
They seem to know 'tis Sabbath day,
And join to sing a grateful lay
　　To HIM who made them all.

Flowers seem more fair, and grass more green,
And trees assume a nobler mien,
　　As if in new array ;
Strange semblance of a richer dress,
As though they did fresh charms possess
　　On every Sabbath day.

The music of that bubbling brook,
Which gently laves the sheltered nook,
  And mirrors objects near ;
Sounds more melodious on this day ;
As it pursues its constant way
  It charms my list'ning ear.

And now I hear the Sabbath bell,
Its cheering sound, and solemn knell,
  Oft fall upon the ear ;
They come from yonder ancient fane,
Where gospel truth is preached quite plain,
  While list'ning mortals hear.

Vast multitudes now wend their way,
To hear the word, and praise, and pray,
  'Neath various hallowed domes ;
The children and their aged sire,
The rich and poor in best attire,
  Alike now leave their homes.

This " pearl of days " may I observe,
And through its sacred moments serve
  The God of earth and heaven ;
Through life revere his holy name,
His glory be my constant aim,
  My all to Him be given.

And when on me heaven's Sabbath dawns,
May I, amid yon shining ones,
  Ascribe unending praise
To Him, whose boundless love to man,
Devised redemption's wondrous plan,
  For every tribe and race.

A Sabbath Evening in Summer.

SABBATH, thy bright, benignant reign,
Is once more near its close again,
   And all thy hallowed sweets
So dear to every Christian's heart,
We must with them a short time part,
   And with thy blest retreats.

Thy priv'leges and welcome rest,
With which we have this day been blest,
   Demand a grateful lay
To HIM, who planned this sweet repose,
And from the grave triumphant rose,
   Upon this blessed day.

The sun now sheds his parting light,
The atmosphere is warm and bright,
   The sky, like burnished gold ;
The clouds present a crimson hue,
With strips of polished white and blue ;
   What grandeur they unfold !

And lo ! I see a lonely star,
In brilliancy transcending far
   The richest gems of earth ;
Scarce brighter was the star which brought
The *wise men*, who the Saviour sought,
   And hailed his royal birth !

The Sabbath bells no longer ring,
The feather'd-choirs have ceased to sing,
   And wait the morning light ;
A purling brook alone I hear,
Its mellow tone delights my ear,
   Amid the shades of night.

Yes, e'en the ocean seems to sleep,
A perfect calm pervades the deep,
   As when, in days of yore,
The Saviour prov'd His sovereign will,
For He but uttered " peace, be still,"
   Which hushed the tempest's roar.

On this blest day the word of truth,
Adapted both to age and youth,
   Again has been proclaimed ;
It has the Christian pilgrim cheered,
(To him more fully now endeared,)
   And erring souls reclaimed.

Around the fam'ly altar now,
Devoutly, Christian households bow,
   And praise HIM who hath given
So many blessings on this day,
To help them on their pilgrim way,
   And make them meet for heaven,

There, one unending Sabbath reigns,
And angels pour harmonious strains,
   Before the great I AM ;
Grief is not felt by one above,
Each heart is filled with purest love,
   To God and to the Lamb.

Autumn.

———

AUTUMN has now its mantle cast
O'er all the earth,—for Summer's past,
  Its sunny smiles and hours ;
And Nature vast assumes a hue
Impressive and instructive too,
  For man's reflective powers.

The ripened grain now ready stands,
And through the day with willing hands
  The reapers ply the hook ;
A kindly word,—a cheerful smile,—
Make labour light and time beguile,
  And thus they happy look.

The farmer's breast with gladness heaves,
As he beholds the golden sheaves,
  And counts them one by one ;
His presence cheers his reaping band,
He gladly lends a helping hand,
  Until the work is done.

Behind, a few are strolling o'er
The fields, like Ruth in days of yore,
  To pick the straggled grain ;
An honourable work is this,
Each spike a precious treasure is,
  To gleaners quite a gain.

Pomona now displays a treat,
For various fruits, both rich and sweet,
    Adorn the trees around ;
Some leaves proclaim that Winter's near,
For they've already turned quite sere,
    And fallen on the ground.

The days are short'ning—nights grow long,
And Autumn winds blow loud and strong,
    Foreboding future ill ;
Along the hills and water's side
At early morn and eventide,
    The atmosphere is chill.

The flowers which did the earth adorn,
Whose fragrance on the breeze was borne
    While Flora's reign did last—
All beautiful, and rich, and gay,
'Mong which the children lov'd to play,
    Are gone,—their season's past.

The russet dell and imbrowned grove,
Where num'rous silenced warblers rove,
    Are changed by Autumn's reign,
From cheerful green to gloomy shade,
Also the pleasant rural glade,
    And every hill and plain.

How great the change from Summer's bloom !
Monotony in all its gloom
    Reigns everywhere around ;
Sometimes a dense and watery fog
Arises from yon sheltered bog,
    And spreads along the ground.

In yonder park deciduous trees
Are shaken by the passing breeze,
   And cast their leaves around ;
Their colours varied, rich, and sweet,
To artists offering quite a treat,
   Which nowhere else is found.

Leaves richly purple, brown, and red,
Some nicely mottled,—some quite dead,
   Some dark and others pale ;
Some still are dangling on the boughs,
And these their altitude will lose,
   Nip'd by the northern gale.

True emblems these of man's short day,
However sprightly, blithe, and gay,
   They represent us all ;
In days of yore the prophet said,
" Just like a leaf we all do fade,"
   And like it soon shall fall.

A woodman's axe is plainly heard,
And fills with fear the lonely bird,
   Which dreads impending harm ;
His steady strokes sound through the wood,
And trees which have for ages stood,
   Fall 'neath his potent arm.

The Squirrel leaps from tree to tree,
The Hare is browsing on the lea,
   And Reynard near the brook ;
A constant watch the spaniel keeps,
His master harkens, lurks and creeps,
   Around the sheltered nook.

A rustic youth with nutting sack
Slung loosely, hanging on his back,
    Is roaming through the wood ;
He shakes the trees, and nuts quite brown,
In great profusion tumble down,
    All fully ripe and good.

But hark ! I hear a warlike sound,
Which makes the hills and dales resound,
    Lo ! too, a howling cry !
It is the huntsman's horn I hear,
Who with his hounds pursues the Deer,
    O'er hedge and ditch they fly.

And now, I see the timid Hare,
In terror flying from its lair,
    To seek a safer spot ;
Poor Puss ! thy life is dear to thee,
And hence thou dost from danger flee ;
    May safety be thy lot.

Some feathered songsters silent are,
Their joys are past when trees are bare,
    And now in Autumn time
The Redstart, Swallow, Blackcap, Quail,
Wild-duck, and Crane, defy the gale,
    And seek a warmer clime.

These birds migrate from shore to shore,
And neither dread the tempest's roar,
    Nor fear so long a flight ;
As seasons change they know the time
To seek a more congenial clime,
    Where all is warm and bright.

Ye wand'ring birds! O, how I love
To watch your flight as on ye move
   To sunny groves and plains ;
True emblems of the Christian here,
Who hastens to yon glorious sphere,
   Where endless Summer reigns.

The Partridge, Pheasant, Lapwing, Crow,
Remain with us through Winter's snow,
   And seek their food with care ;
But some, perchance, next Summer's sun
May never see,—the sportsman's gun
   Will not the choicest spare.

More frequent now the Robin comes
Beside our cots, to pick the crumbs,
   And tunes his ruby throat ;
He's left the woods, for Winter's near,
And gladly comes our days to cheer
   With his melodious note.

Blithe little bird ! thy lays are sweet,
Affording us a welcome treat
   When Summer's joys are o'er ;
While other birds have crossed the main,
With us thou choosest to remain,
   And sing beside our door.

A ploughman plods his weary way,
He hums a tune the livelong day
   Whilst turning up the earth ;
And soon he'll sow the precious grain,
Which, watered by soft showers of rain,
   Will in due time spring forth.

Huge sombre clouds are floating there,
Rendering dark the atmosphere,
   And wear a threat'ning form ;
The Crows are flying near the ground,
And other birds have shelter found
   Against the coming storm.

That Winter's storms will soon betide
The flocks upon the mountain's side,
   They seem full well to know ;
For now they keep more close together,
Than they are wont in Summer-weather,
   When gentle breezes blow.

Lo ! now the patt'ring rain descends,
And with its sound Boreas blends
   A harsh, discordant blast ;
Loud thunder rolls above my head,
And light'nings glare,—while filled with dread,
   Men wish the storm were past.

Autumn ! thy charms are few indeed,
And ought our thoughtful minds to lead,
   In contemplating man ;
He, who now is past mature age,
And 'proximates tow'rds Winter's stage,
   Enfeebl'd much and wan.

Yes, Autumn is a picture true
Of man's decline, when joys are few,
   And fleeting manhood's bloom ;
When age its with'ring influence shows,
And man with falt'ring footsteps goes
   To meet his final doom.

The Christian only comfort feels
As Autumn o'er him gently steals,
   And damps his earthly bliss ;
His hope is full—his prospect bright,
His soul exults to take its flight,
   To dwell where Jesus is.

In him the Spirit's fruits are seen,
All fully ripe,—his leaf is green,
   Much grace to him is given ;
Engrafted in the Living Vine,
And ever fill'd with love divine
   Made fully meet for heaven,

For yonder cloudless, deathless clime,
Untouch'd by human hands and time,
   And lit with glorious rays ;
Where bloom ambrosial flowers and fruit,
And angels tune the golden lute,
   And on the Saviour gaze.

A Morning in Autumn.

With joy I hail Aurora's reign,
Again she smiles o'er hill and plain,
   But frigid is her breath ;
Nature assumes a dusky hue,
Declining verdure greets the view,
   And leaflets sink in death.

How powerless now are Sol's bright beams !
Through watery clouds his lustre gleams,
   And passing showers of rain ;
At noon itself he faintly shines,
His rays are shed in feeble lines
   O'er Nature's wide domain.

The wind is moaning round my head,
A requiem for the Summer fled ;
   How dismal is its tone !
The little brooklet, late so bright,
No longer sparkles in the light,
   While rippling o'er each stone.

Those trees have lost their verdant dress,
The hedges now no charms possess,
   Through them the north winds sigh ;
How lonely seems that little bird,
How seldom too a chirp is heard,
   Except when danger's nigh.

Some noisy Rooks on yonder tree,
Perchance some distant danger see,
   How great the din they make !
Yes, now a sportsman's gun I hear,
And birds are flying full of fear,
   From tree, and bush, and brake.

Though night is pass'd, deep gloom prevails,
And Autumn's store now quickly fails,
   Drear Winter's close at hand ;
The river's gush sounds dismal still,
And beauty's fled from vale and hill,
   As by a magic wand.

These leaves which do my path o'erspread,
Though lately verdant—now quite dead,
　　Will quickly disappear :
E'en so will man, as seasons roll,
Decline in strength, and fin'lly fall,
　　He's but a pilgrim here.

Grasp'd by the icy hand of death,
The Christian yields his vital breath,
　　And disappears from sight :
His body moulders 'neath the sod,
His spirit dwells with Saints and God,
　　In yonder realms of light.

An Evening in Autumn.

'Tis eve, and as through fields I walk,
I hear anon the Raven's croak
　　From yon old pile remote ;
And now a Sparrow hears my tread,
And quickly lifting up his head,
　　He chirps a warning note.

Replace thy head behind thy wing,
Thou little, fearful, helpless thing,
　　And do not heed my tread ;
A Sparrow does the notice share
Of Him, who here could find nowhere
　　To rest His sacred head.

How chill the air and damp the ground,
As Nox her mantle spreads around,
  And objects hides from sight ;
The stars are hid by watery clouds,
And darkness—earth and sky enshrouds,
  With scarce one streak of light.

Rain-drops are falling here and there,
From twigs which can't their pressure bear,
  And make a trickling sound ;
The wind is moaning round the eaves,
And stirs the corrugated leaves
  Which overspread the ground.

How dismal, too, yon river's flow,
Its sound is sadd'ning, deep, and low,
  Amid the shades of night ;
A constant, hollow, death-like boom
Augments the universal gloom,
  Pressing my spirits quite.

But hark ! a screeching sound is heard,
It comes from some voracious bird,
  While searching for its prey ;
Its savage screams the flocks now hear,
They're bleating loud, all fill'd with fear,
  As well indeed they may.

My wand'ring steps I'll now retrace,
And seek a more congenial place,
  Till morning smiles anew ;
The moaning wind and rustling leaves,
Unnerve my frame like nightly thieves,
  And it with fear imbue.

But why afraid? Jehovah's nigh,
Who made the ocean, earth and sky,
    And He in keeping hath
My all, by night as well as day,
Yes, e'en when not a single ray
    Of light illumes my path.

Winter.

How dark and drear all Nature seems,
The rivers, lakes, and winding streams,
    With ice are cover'd o'er!
The lofty hills are clad with snow,
And chilling blasts with fury blow
    Along the ocean's shore.

Phœbus has now reached *Capricorn*,
And of his strength is greatly shorn,
    His disc but dimly glows;
The atmosphere is seldom bright,
Keen frost prevails both day and night,
    Its power all Nature shows.

Oft when Aurora takes her place,
All Nature wears a silvery face,
    And sparkles in the light;
But Phœbus' beams the charm dispels,
His power upon the hoar-frost tells,—
    Which disappears from sight.

The barren earth and stormy main,
Alike proclaim drear Winter's reign,
   O'er all his mantle's cast ;
Both day and night his influence show,
And round our cots the north winds blow
   A loud and angry blast.

The chirping Sparrow seeks our door,
And when he's fed he chirps the more,
   How truly pleased is he !
The Magpie and the Jay laid by
A Winter-store for their supply,
   In some old hollow tree.

The clam'rous Rooks in search of food,
Have left the naked barren wood,
   And scour the country o'er ;
Along the coast the Corm'rant flies,
Mingling his doleful, piercing cries,
   With wind and ocean's roar,

The Snipe and Woodcock now are here,
They've come to spend the Winter drear,
   While Summer-birds have fled ;
And when bright Spring returns again,
These Winter-birds will cross the main,
   By strangest instinct led.

On yonder pond the skaters hie,
And some are swiftly gliding by
   Without the aid of skates ;
The traveller plods his weary way,
The snow keeps falling all the day
   In large and blinding flakes.

The oak though late arrayed in green,
Without a single leaf is seen,
   For every twig is bare ;
Also the various shrubs and trees
Which spread their fragrance on the breeze,
   Quite faded now they are.

The humble box lifts up its head
Above the snow which clothes its bed,
   Its verdure never dies ;
The ivy too its freshness keeps,
Along the wall it gently creeps,
   And every storm defies.

The Lark no longer soars on high,
Or pours with such an ecstacy
   His sweet and cheering lay ;
The Linnet warbles not his song,
In trees and arborets among,
   So merry and so gay.

And while the snow o'erspreads the ground,
The little Redbreast flies around
   Our cots,—by hunger led ;
He sings all day, though cold it be,
And seems so full of mirth and glee,
   When he with crumbs is fed.

The tiny golden-crested Wren
Is flying up and down the glen,
   In search of Winter-fare ;
The Titmouse too on airy wing,
Visits the garden, field, and spring,
   And seeks its food with care.

With tatter'd clothes and visage wan,
There goes a poor old beggar man,
   Almost benumbed with cold ;
Children are making balls of snow,
And these at passers-by they throw,
   Annoying young and old.

Some boys have made a monster ball,
Which larger grows as on they roll
   The high and pond'rous mass ;
With strength united—minds agreed,
They make the mountain-ball proceed,
   And thus their time they pass.

Perchance upon the mountain's side,
The drifts of snow both deep and wide
   Will every track efface ;
And travellers strive and strive again,
But all their efforts prove in vain,
   To reach their destin'd place.

Pedestrians have midst Winter's snows,
Experienc'd all the direful woes,
   With which they do abound ;
The cold has quench'd the vital flame,
And stretch'd in death, the stiffen'd frame,
   Has on the snow been found.

Anon we have a gentle thaw,
Which soon dissolves the ice and snow,
   And fructifies the ground ;
And then is heard the creak and crash
Of breaking ice, and furious dash
   Of waters lately bound.

The melting snow and falling rain,
Do sometimes inundate the plain,
   And spread alarm around ;
The river too, and lake, and rill,
O'erflow their banks, and help to fill
   The low and marshy ground.

Amidst the gloom of Winter's reign,
When snow o'erspreads both hill and plain,
   And nights are dark and long ;
Old Christmas comes with all his cheer,
To many hearts his charms are dear,
   He's hail'd by old and young.

This merry friend is close at hand,
And here and there a youthful band,
   Will gather round the fire :
Enigmas make and stories tell,
And then their cheerful voices swell
   In one harmonious choir.

Such is bluff Winter's frigid reign,
'Tis felt alike on land and main,
   How piercing is his blast !
His form is gaunt, and wan his face ;
His mantle white, worn with a grace,
   Is now o'er Nature cast.

But Winter drear will soon be past,
For cheerful Spring approaches fast,
   When flowers will deck the plains ;
And trees will bud and blossom fair,
And warbling songsters fill the air
   With sweet, melodious strains.

E'en so does life's short Wintry-day
Keep gliding rapidly away,
  But *never to return ;*
To some, perchance, 'twill close in night,
To others, in the glorious light
  Of an immortal morn.

Winter, thy cold and cheerless state,
Precisely represents the fate
  Of him whose end is near ;
Whose life-blood freezes in his veins,
And who, while on the earth remains,
  Is dead to all things here.

The aged man with silvery hair,
And who his frame can scarcely bear,
  And leans upon his staff,
Has now arrived at Winter's stage,
His body's wrinkled o'er with age,
  Earth's joys he cannot quaff.

When Nature's spent, and days are few,
And dissolution just in view,
  The Christian's not alone ;
For angels wait to waft his soul
To yonder happy, peaceful goal,
  Where Winter is unknown.

Bright, joyous, endless Spring will come,
And round the Christian's path will bloom
  Perennial fruits and flowers ;
Grief cannot mar an angel's face,
Storms cannot reach that heavenly place,
  To blast its golden bowers.

A Morning in Winter.

THE hush of night has pass'd away,
And now Aurora leads the way,
  Diffusing light around ;
The stars are hid from mortal sight,
Horus ascends his wonted height,
  And man at toil is found.

King Frost his potent sway maintains,
He still o'er hill and valley reigns,
  And binds the rippling brook ;
The torrent by his breath is hush'd,
Which down the mountain wildly rush'd,
  And neighb'ring objects shook.

Huge icicles are hanging there,
And things are frozen everywhere,
  How biting is the cold ;
And on the window pane we see—
Sketch'd by King Frost,—a flower—a tree,
  How curious to behold !

Yon boys, while on their way to school,
Feel sensibly their ardour cool,
  And breathe upon their fingers ;
Arriv'd at school, the blazing hearth
Is soon besieg'd, where, fill'd with mirth,
  Each boy most gladly lingers.

Lo ! now hailstones are rattling round,
Which shine like spangles on the ground,
   And dance like things of life ;
They're diamonds set on Winter's dress,
And num'rous mystic charms possess,
   With peerless beauty rife.

The birds are seeking shelter now,
And quickly fly from bough to bough,
   As if they fear'd some harm ;
The Robin, with his crimson breast,
Seems wiser far than all the rest,
   He's fled to yonder farm.

Anon the sun sheds forth his beams,
But few and feeble are his gleams,
   He seems afraid to shine ;
King Frost defies Sol's latent power,
And gath'ring clouds above me lower,
   And hail and snow combine.

E'en when the sun at noonday shines,
His oblique rays in feeble lines
   Fall powerless on the ground ;
And soon he hides again his face,
Nor of his reign leaves any trace
   On vegetation round.

How bracing is the passing breeze,
It does the human system seize,
   And all its powers defy ;
Now whistles loud—then moans awhile,
Moving trees in furious style,
   And clouds across the sky,

The frost though keen, and stiff the breeze,
The brook though still, and bare the trees,
   And feather'd-songsters dumb ;
It is Jehovah's fixed decree,
That seasons shall not cease to be,
   Hence, Spring again will come.

An Evening in Winter.

THE lengthen'd night has clos'd around,
And as I tread the snow-clad ground,
   I feel the chilling breeze ;
Envelop'd in my Winter-cloak,
I quite enjoy this evening walk,
   Though keen the north-winds freeze.

The frozen snow creaks 'neath my tread,
Like polish'd gems my path o'erspread,
   And radiate the ground :
The trees and hedges rob'd anew,
Bend 'neath the snow, and sparkle too,
   And brightness shed around.

What stillness reigns ! how great the hush !
I miss the pleasant, laughing gush
   Of yonder limpid rill ;
King Frost has lock'd it in his arms,
And robb'd it of its num'rous charms,
   Its waters now are still.

The whistling blasts which round me blow,
My footsteps on the frozen snow,
   Are all the sounds I hear ;
E'en now the most voracious bird,
Which nightly screams, cannot be heard,
   All, all is still and drear.

Myriads of shining stars on high,
Bedeck the blue ether'al sky,
   And strike with awe profound,
The Christian's mind, who loves to scan
The works of God in Nature's plan,
   Throughout Creation's bound.

The polar-star,—" the Queen of Night,"—
And milky-way with radiance bright,
   Almighty power display !
Some planets shine with steady light,
Some stars keep twinkling all the night,
   Till lost in opening day,

To these the Royal Psalmist rais'd
His wond'ring eyes, and while he gaz'd
   He saw the hand divine ;
" The heavens declare thy glory, Lord,"
He cried, and thus with joy ador'd
   The God that made them shine

The sailor on the stormy deep,
Does through the night a vigil keep,
   And steers his gallant barque ;
The polar-star he loves to see,
It guides him o'er the wide, wide sea,
   However wild and dark.

The biting frost—the fleecy snow—
The piercing, veering blasts which blow,
    God's love to man declare ;
They're sent to fructify the ground,
Make it with charms in Spring abound,
    And purify the air.

But now I'll leave this lonely spot,
And hasten to my welcome cot,
    Where study, time beguiles ;
First, by the ingle take my seat
Then to a safe and snug retreat
    Retire, till morning smiles.

—:o:—

MISCELLANEOUS.

—:o:—

NATIONAL.

—:o:—

Stanzas to Great Britain.

O LAND of my fathers,—the home of the free,
Renown'd in all countries,—the gem of the sea ;
Many nations admire thy insular shore,
Where Neptune's proud billows unceasingly roar.

Thy army and navy are loyal and brave,
Regardless of danger their country to save :
The SPANISH ARMADA that came against thee,
Was quickly dispers'd,—overthrown on the sea.

Thy Administration,—our glory and pride !
For *justice to all* is our bulwark and guide ;
Thy Monarch's mild sceptre,—thy Counsellors great,
Thy National Church,—all give power to the state.

Thy unbounded riches,—thy treasures of lore,
Thy hives of industry,—thy mines of rich ore ;
Thy climate salubrious,—each valley and hill,
With proud admiration thy patriots fill.

Thy wide-spreading forests,—thy gardens and bowers
Embellish'd with myriads of sweet-scented flowers ;
Thy landscapes so varied,—thy pastures so green,
Thy rivers so limpid are sparkling with sheen.

Thy Commerce is great on the ocean and land,
Thy railways so num'rous,—thy shipping so grand ;
Thy merchants so wealthy, so upright, and true,
Secure from all nations, respect which is due.

The arts and the sciences flourish around,
In some of thy cities there's classical ground ;
The Bible is honour'd, its truths are made known—
The secret of strength to the state and the throne.

Thy noble asylums,—how num'rous and vast !
Befriending the orphan and helpless outcast ;
For these thy philanthropists frequently plead,
And cheerfully labour to meet every need.

Thy castles in ruins, and abbeys of yore,
With turrets and battlements crumbling and hoar,
Around which the ivy luxuriantly twines,
Have histories in which true chivalry shines.

Thy august Cathedrals,—embellish'd by art,
The pride of our cities,—the joy of our heart ;
Encompass'd by Churches of lowlier mien,
All add to the glory of Britain's fair Queen.

Thy long line of worthies,—illustrious and great,
For ages adorning the Church and the State ;
With SHAKSPEARE and MILTON, of world-wide renown,
Are stars in thy hemisphere all nations own.

A Protestant people ! intelligent, bold,
Who love *truth* and *freedom* far more than fine gold ;
Whose forefathers died in defence of the same,
Defying the Pope, and the rack, and the flame.

Thy prestige is envied by people afar,
Thy glory transcends the most luminous star ;
Thy language is spoken in far distant climes,
Thy prowess is felt in all countries and times.

Hurrah for Great Britain ! she has no compeer,
Her annals illustrious—her memory dear—
To thousands who've proved her both gen'rous and brave,
A foe to the tyrant,—a friend to the slave.

Hurrah for Victoria ! our well-beloved Queen,
Hurrah for her family ! who always have been
The patrons of science, religion, and lore,
God bless them, yea, bless them, a thousand times o'er.

The Queen.—A Sonnet.

TRUE womanly grace and royal mien,
Embellish the life of Britain's Queen ;
The brightness of her glorious reign,
Is shed over lands across the main ;
And England,—prosperous—noble—free,
Under her sceptre shall ever be
Contented ;—and may her regal line
Continuously with lustre shine,
    A pattern to the imperial race.
And may the nations both far and near,
VICTORIA'S power and name revere ;
    In all her actions and statutes trace
    Right, justice, and freedom, truth, and grace,
And like herself the Almighty fear.

A Dirge on the Death of Prince Albert,

Which took place December 14th, 1861.

—

ALBERT THE GOOD,—thy loss we mern,
  And all are bow'd with grief!
Stricken our hearts,—quite sad and lern ;
  Thy earthly life how brief!

Thy Royal Consort weeps for thee,
  Thy children's grief is great ;
And people own most mournfully,
  Thy loss to Church and State.

Thy noble heart and gifted mind,
  From earth have pass'd away ;
And mingle now with souls refined,
  In realms of cloudless day.

Our harps are on the willows hung,
  No gladsome sound is heard :
Each heart with sorrow is unstrung,
  The Nation's heart is stirr'd.

O God ! thy chastisements are just,
  Inflicted one by one ;
May we all learn in Thee to trust,
  And say " Thy will be done."

May we have grace to kiss the rod
  Which has been wisely used :
And seek forgiveness from our God,
  Whose gifts we have abused.

Epithalamium;

OR,

Lines on the Marriage of the Prince of Wales,

MARCH 10TH, 1863.

For which the Author received the thanks of His Royal Highness.

———

LET every British heart rejoice,
And strains of rapture tune each voice,
On this eventful day of days,
Where'er VICTORIA'S sceptre sways.

For England's hope, and England's pride,
To-day receives his royal bride ;
A Danish Princess,—pure, serene,
Old England's future charming Queen.

A general holiday proclaim,
Let loyalty each breast enflame ;
And pray, " God bless in yonder fane,
The English Prince and Royal Dane."

Let thousands, dress'd in best attire,
Who Prince and Princess much admire,
Wear white rosettes and flow'rets gay,
On this their happy wedding day.

Ring, ring the bells throughout the land,
Let organs peal with music grand ;
And cannon loud from every fort,
The tidings far and wide report.

Let bands of music march along,
And echoes still their strains prolong ;
From hill to hill, and through the vales
Be heard, " God bless the Prince of Wales."

Let festoon'd arches span each street,
In which both skill and beauty meet ;
There, " Long live Prince of Wales," appear,
And " Welcome Danish Princess " here.

Let ships in every harbour vie
With colours hoisted top-mast high ;
And houses deck'd in like array,
To celebrate this nuptial day.

On every railway train and station,
All throughout the British nation,
Let banners float,—along the rails
Be heard, " God bless the Prince of Wales."

At night illuminate the land
With torches, rockets, bonfires grand ;
And let the houses all display
Most brilliant lights to close the day.

Let Englishmen and Danes unite
To render great this bond so bright ;
And may each nation, strong and free,
Be ever blest, O God, by Thee.

On the Birth of a Prince.

JANUARY 8TH, 1864.

HARK ! hark ! the bells are ringing,
   Throughout this sea-girt isle ;
Pure joy is upward springing,
   In every heart the while ;
All hail the bright auspicious morn
Which brings the news,—a Prince is born.

Loud, loud is cannon thund'ring
   From every British fort ;
While multitudes are wond'ring,
   Report succeeds report :
On every breeze the news is borne,—
An English Prince and Heir is born.

See, see the flags are flying,
   O what a rich display !
Both old and young are vieing
   To celebrate the day,—
And houses, ships, and forts adorn,
Because a Prince and Heir is born.

Let, let us all be pleading,
   That gifts without alloy,
From heaven each day succeeding,
   May rest upon this boy ;
And also rest upon his sire,
Whom every Briton must admire.

Bless, bless the royal mother,
　　May grace to her be given,
As days succeed each other,
　　To train her babe for heaven ;
And long may peace and plenty reign
Throughout VICTORIA'S vast domain.

On the Death of Princess Alice,

December 14th, 1878.

A NOBLE heart has ceased to beat,
　　A noble soul has pass'd away ;
Such true nobility was meet
　　To dwell in realms of endless day.

Whilst here midst royalty she dwelt,
　　And dazzling splendours daily shared ;
But nothing she possess'd or felt,
　　Can with Heaven's glories be compared.

And now those glories she inherits,
　　Which nought can dim or take away ;
Secured to her through Jesu's merits,
　　In mansions where there's no decay.

Dire sickness often did invade
　　The palace where her children slept ;
And Death to one a visit paid,
　　Whilst over her the Princess wept.

And now, O Death ! thy poisonous dart
    Has been directed towards another ;
For thou hast pierced the loving heart
    Of her who was *so true a mother.*

Well may the Queen of England mourn
    For her lov'd one—the Princess Alice ;
And all hearts be with anguish torn,
    In every cottage, hall, and palace,

No earthly pomp, nor robes of state,
    No august throne, nor jewell'd crown,
Can shield a prince or potenate
    From Death, whose power all men must own.

But there's a better world above
    Where nothing shall our spirits harm ;
There all shall dwell in peace and love,
    For ever safe from Death's alarm.

On the Death of Prince Leopold, Duke of Albany,

WHICH TOOK PLACE AT CANNES, MARCH 28TH, 1884.

A PRINCE is dead ! a nation mourns
    One worthy of his princely sire !
Whose life our national page adorns—
    Whose words and deeds we all admire.

Leopold, Duke of Albany !
    The idol of his Royal mother ;
A model son ! no wonder she
    Admired him more than any other.

Well may she weep for one most dear,
    Her loss so great can not be told ;
His heart so loving—mind so clear—
    Were more to her than heaps of gold.

The Duchess, too, has felt the stroke,
    For from her side her stay is taken ;
But comforted by Him who spoke,—
    " Thou shalt not be by Me forsaken."

Far distant, in a foreign land,
    Death, cruel Death, his victim took ;
Nor wife, nor mother, close at hand,
    To whom the Prince for help could look.

But God was nigh, and with his grace
    Sustained his mind, as there he lay
Upon his couch, with no loved face
    To cheer his heart from day to day.

Lo ! now in heaven the Prince appears,
    A golden crown adorns his brow :
No fear of death, no pain, no tears,
    Afflict his ransomed spirit now.

A sceptre, throne, and harp are his,
    A robe of pure unsullied white ;
And with unnumbered hosts in bliss,
    Experiences untold delight.

Our loss of him is his great gain !
    Yes, gain through one eternal day :—
All fun'ral pomp is worthless—vain—
    And all the honours we can pay.

May Queen Victoria rise to reign
    In bliss supreme, and see him there ;
And may the Duchess once again
    Join him, true happiness to share !

London.

O CITY of wonders, of wealth, and of fame !
   Within thy vast precincts I stand—
In London ! yes, London ! how charming the name,
Enchanting to youth, and to old age the same,
   The glory and pride of our land.

Some cities may boast of extensive renown,
   And really marvellous appear ;
But what are their merits compared with thine own ?
In commerce and magnitude so overgrown,
   'Mong cities thou hast no compeer.

How countless the multitudes thronging thy streets,
   Nor ceasing from morning till night !
Thy gigantic heart full of life ever beats,
Each day and each hour thy history repeats,
   A history of dark shades and light.

Thy noble Cathedral with pleasure I view,
   And admire its statuary rare ;
Its tablets so varied—some old and some new—
On which are inscribed names of patriots true,
   My careful attention now share.

From the dome of St. Paul I look all around,
   And witness a scene unsurpassed ;
I fail to distinguish the uttermost bound
Of the buildings which this fine temple surround,
   And cannot be numbered nor class'd.

A continuous din comes up from below,
  Assailing most strangely mine ear—
A sound as if caused by the ocean's hoarse flow,
Or some mighty river, quite angry and slow,
  Exciting both wonder and fear.

The Thames, with its unnumbered barges, I see,
  And steam-packets moving along ;
Its wharfs and its bridges to strangers must be
Attractive—as also amusing to me,
  So grotesque and motley the throng.

The Parliament Houses I gaze on awhile—
  Their unrivalled splendour admire !
No city can boast of a more noble pile,
Not more truly splendid, more royal in style :
  What more can a Briton desire ?

And not far away stands the Abbey of yore,
  Where Royalty oft has been crowned :
And multitudes wander most reverently o'er
Its transepts and chapels, intent to explore
  The objects of interest around.

There lie the remains of great monarchs of old,
  Whose histories live with us still :
And of their exploits we have often been told—
They revelled midst luxurious pleasures and gold,
  And ruled with inflexible will.

The hoary old Tower of London I spy,
  Where Royalty oft was immured ;
There nobles, and ladies, and others most high
In station and office were led forth to die,
  And darkest of deeds were endured.

The British Museum must not be forgot,
  So fraught with historical lore :
Attracting some hundreds each day to the spot
To look upon things—quite a curious lot—
  A rare and invaluable store.

The Palaces of our lov'd Queen are quite near—
  Their environs are beauteous and grand ;
And these have to Britons attractions most dear,
Who pray that Victoria may reign without fear,
  And long may she live in the land.   ·

O city of cities ! thy blessings are great—
  Thy people exalted and free :
The Bible is honoured by thy Protentate,
Religion's the bulwark of Church and of State,
  And nations thy glory all see.

Impromptu :

Suggested by the marvellous recovery of the Prince of Wales from
a dangerous illness, in answer to a Nation's prayer.

THE heart of the Nation was deeply mov'd
With pity, for one for whom it behov'd
That prayer should be made, to HIM who can save,
Yes, e'en from the brink of the yawning grave.
Unconscious the suff'rer lay on his bed,
While blessings were sought to rest on his head ;
And HE, who did king Hezekiah restore,
Heard and answer'd,—as oft HE had done before:
In mercy to us, the Prince HE did spare,—
How wondrous the power of a Nation's prayer !

LOCAL.

—

The Black Country.

—

O ENGLISHMEN, give ear,
O men, both far and near,
    In town and city,
    Unto my ditty !
O men of England hear :—
    Black—black—black
Is the country round about ;
    Black—black—black
Are some people out and out ;
But then it is no disgrace
At a proper time and place,
To have begrimed hands and face,
    And a weary head and back.

    Smoke—smoke—smoke
From thousands of chimneys flies ;
    Smoke—smoke—smoke
Oft hides from our gaze the skies ;
Enveloping lab'ring crowds,
And towns and villages shrouds :
O dear ! these horrible clouds,
    Men blacken and almost choke.

    Soot—soot—soot
Incessantly falls around ;
    Soot—soot—soot
Besmears and darkens the ground ;

The laundry-maid's clothes are soiled,
Efforts to whiten are foiled,
The gardener's flowers are spoiled
　　By this continual smut.

Dust—dust—dust,
　Yes, plenty of dust forsooth !
Dust—dust—dust
　Will enter your eyes and mouth ;
And oft like a swarm of bees,
Around you will twirl, and seize
Your nostrils, making you sneeze,
　　When roused by a veering gust.

Dirt—dirt—dirt
　Our toiling artizan cloys ;
Dirt—dirt—dirt
　Bespatters both girls and boys.
Some men feel perfectly right,
From morning till late at night,
Though in a comical plight,
　　Denuded of vest and shirt.

Work—work—work,
　Yes, this is the place for toil ;
Work—work—work,
　Above and below the soil ;
Some hands turn clay into brick,
And others to iron stick,
While miners black diamonds pick
　　Where they in abundance lurk.

Wage—wage—wage,
　Is the lab'ring man's request ;
Wage—wage—wage,
　And plenty of time for rest :

Give wages sufficient, give,
O let him have means to live,
And often a kind reprieve
    Bestow upon youth and age.

Britons shall not be slaves,
On land or ocean's waves,
    In city or town,
    And thus be brought down
To fill untimely graves.
    Slaves—slaves—slaves,
No, not in this land so free ;
    Slaves—slaves—slaves,
Never, no never can be,—
And none like a lazy Turk,
In silence and secret lurk ;
A Briton will gladly work,
    For which he good wages craves.

Craves—craves—craves,
But not with a miser's heart ;
Craves—craves—craves,
That he may blessings impart ;
He blesses his fam'ly dear,
And then with a mind sincere,
For many good objects near—
    To help he carefully saves.

Hurrah ! hurrah for England !
Along its shores and inland,—
    The people are free
    As the bird and bee,
    Which rove o'er the lea ;
Hurrah ! hurrah for England !

Loyal and brave,
On land and wave,
All cry, " God save,
And bless the Queen of England :"
And through the Black Country round,
Large churches and schools are found,
Bibles and Christians abound,
Hurrah ! hurrah for England !

The City of Lichfield.

(Written during the Author's residence at Lichfield College,
in 1870.)

BARDS oft have sung of classic Greece,
   Of Roman lore and wonders,
Of arts, philosophy, and peace,
   Of skilful deeds and blunders ;
Of signs above and scenes below,
   Of battle fields all gory,
Of thousands stricken down with woe,
   And thousands flush'd with glory.

But I'll not sing of Greece or Rome,
   Nor yet of eastern sages ;
I'll tell of something near my home,
   Which oft my mind engages ;
Of nature, art, religion too,
   (An interesting ditty),
For sweetly mingling here, they do
   Adorn this ancient city.

All round, through meads profusely spread
  With buttercups and daisies,
Enchanting walks invite my tread,
  Presenting varied phases ;
The hedgegrows deck'd with noble trees,
  The ground quite undulating ;
And from the pools a gentle breeze
  Induces ambulating.

Sweet Minster pool ! thy waves reflect
  Some objects worthy noting,—
Shrubs, trees, and spires all intersect
  Where graceful Swans are floating :
And on thy banks soft strains are heard,
  For feather'd tribes are singing ;
And now, as if to help each bird,
  Cathedral bells are ringing.

Within that grand old fane so rare,
  Replete with Gothic beauty,
Is heard the voice of praise and prayer,
  A daily Christian duty :
The Bishop's Palace is close by,
  The College too, and Deanery ;
And Stowe-pool promenade is nigh,
  'Mid varied woodland scenery.

Burroughcop Hill, of some renown,
  For there the Christian martyr
Died for the truth,*—is near the town,
  And in the southern quarter :
From thence is seen a landscape fair,
  Extensive—varied—charming ;
With signs of plenty everywhere,
  The fruits of skilful farming.

---

* *See Harwood's History of Lichfield, page* 561.

Among the churches of the town,
　St. Chad's claims special mention ;
As foremost of antique renown,
　Well worthy of attention.
St. Mary's, too,—a noble pile,—
　A credit to the people,
Of recent date, and modern style,
　With lofty spiral steeple.

St. Michael's church since days of yore,
　To benefit immortals,
Has welcomed all, both rich and poor,
　Within its sacred portals.
A Mausoleum greets mine eye,
　'Tis by a clock surmounted,
Reminding all that death is nigh,
　And time by moments counted.

The city boasts of JOHNSON's birth,
　A scholar— critic—poet ;
The British nation owns his worth,
　And other nations know it :
His house adorns St. Mary's Square,
　A public benefaction ;
His statue too,—of sculpture rare,
　Both objects of attraction.

A free Museum, well supplied
　With fossils, busts, and pictures,
Has coins and insects classified,
　And many strange admixtures ;
Here curious minds obtain full play,
　For objects greatly vary ;
And those of ancient date repay
　The thoughtful antiquary.

A public News-Room,—quite a boon,—
  (Just what some towns are needing),
Is open daily, late and soon,
  For those who're fond of reading :
The Standard, Times, and Telegraph,
  Are laid upon the tables ;
And merry *Punch* to make you laugh
  With car'catures and fables.

Religious privileges abound,
  And schools for youthful training ;
Hospitals for the poor are found,
  And charity's not waning :
The people,—kind, polite,—nay, more,—
  Some well-informed and witty,
Whose consecrated wealth and lore,
  Exalt this loyal city.

The Old Parish Church, Wednesbury,

1872.

Upon the hill,—and pointing high,
With spiral form to yonder sky,
There stands to greet and please the eye,—
        The Old Parish Church.

When dangers threaten all around,
And frank or secret foes abound,
Firmly it stands,—while they surround
        The Old Parish Church.

Dense clouds of smoke on every gale,
The fairest scenes of earth assail ;
But one, to harm they always fail,—
          The Old Parish Church.

Once superstition reigned around,
And Druids worshipped on this ground,
Their priests oft stood where now is found
          The Old Parish Church.

When Druid-rites had passed away,
A Castle, with its turrets grey,
Adorned the site where now we pray,
          In the Old Parish Church.

Year after year roll'd on awhile,
And then a fane of gothic style
Rose up,—this noble, sacred pile,—
          The Old Parish Church.

Stained-glass windows and tablets rare,
Marble figures recumbent there,
All beautify this house of prayer,—
          The Old Parish Church.

In sunshine, and when tempests lower,
The four-faced clock proclaims each hour,
To people, from the time-worn tower
          Of the Old Parish Church.

That life is short and death is nigh,
Thousands who in the graveyard lie,
Daily remind all passing by
          The Old Parish Church.

Outside and in the Church we gaze
On monuments which speak the praise
Of some, who lov'd, in by-gone days,
        The Old Parish Church.

On Sabbath-days, at stated times,
The belfry pours melodious chimes,
As up the hill each Christian climbs
        To the Old Parish Church.

To hear again the Pastor preach,
Admonish, warn, and plainly teach,
All hasten on,—quite glad to reach,
        The Old Parish Church.

And soon the organ's strains are heard,
Sweet voices join, and hearts are stirr'd
By earnest prayers and faithful word,
        In the Old Parish Church.

May error ne'er the truth displace,
Of Romish ritual be no trace,
Nor Popish vestments e'er disgrace
        The Old Parish Church.

Crosses, candles, and incense may
Suit some whose hearts have gone astray,
But keep, O keep them all away
        From the Old Parish Church.

Christ is the chief attraction there,
Communion sweet his people share
Whene'er they join in praise and prayer
        In the Old Parish Church.

O sacred place ! to thousands dear,
Where many shed affection's tear,
Beside the graves of lov'd ones near
    The Old Parish Church.

Here oft is tied the nuptial knot,
And babes baptized upon this spot ;
Say,—can it ever be forgot—
    The Old Parish Church ?

Of some things,—name, and form, and style,
Are well remember'd for awhile ;
But mem'ry lingers round this pile,
    The Old Parish Church.

As generations onward move,
Mutation seen around—above ;
Unchanged, the heart will fondly love
    The Old Parish Church.

Woodgreen, 1878.

My theme is not lofty,—my words are but few,
My object is worthy,—to render what's due
To a hamlet unknown in the annals of fame,
A suburb of Wednesbury,—Woodgreen is its name.

How lovely to walk by the side of each pool,
While zephyrs are passing,—refreshing and cool ;
How pleasing to witness the Swans' evolutions,
Now floating,—then pluming,—with sundry ablutions.

How charming to stroll where the river Tame glides!
Where Flora now treads, and in beauty presides;
And listen to birds trilling early and late,
While stock-dove and corn-crake each calls for his mate.

Luxuriantly adorned with flowerets so rare,
The Cemetery must our attention now share;
For here Nature and Art most sweetly combine
To render this Charnel-house beauteous and fine.

How num'rous the mounds where the silent dead lie!
And striking the tombstones to each passer by;
All suggesting the thought. (while oft drops a tear),
That life is but short, and that death is quite near.

The homes of the cottagers, cleanly and neat,
And gardens with plants, shrubs, and flowers replete;
Together with mansions all stately and fair,
Whose 'mediate surroundings are lovely and rare.

Most attractive of all is that sacred pile,
But lately erected in true Gothic style;
Where people are bless'd with " the water of life,"
Productive of peace, and the healer of strife.

O may the inhabitants frequently go
To drink of the streams which abundantly flow:
And finally rise to that temple above,
Where myriads now drink of the stream of God's love.

—:():—

On Leaving Wednesbury to Reside at Oakengates, 1879.

Most peculiar indeed are the feelings which rise
  Within,—and my thoughts are unusual, very,
Whilst thinking of many loved friends whom I prize,
  And scenes so familiar in dear Wednesbury.

Peradventure the faces and voices of some
  I no more shall greet in this region of change:
But hope that the time will most certainly come,
  When again we shall meet and no partings exchange.

How oft around Church Hill I've wander'd and mused,
  And gazed upon scenes both painful and pleasant;
Yes, grieved to see Sabbath days greatly abused,
  But pleased in the Church to see worshippers present.

Also to King's Hill I have frequently gone,
  To visit the needy, the sick, and the dying;
And there I've proclaimed that Christ Jesus alone,
  Can pardon the guilty, and comfort the sighing.

Through Woodgreen and round Elwell's pools I have
      strayed,
  And strolled through the meadows away to the
      Delves,
Where songsters have trilled, and the lambkins have
      played,
  And groups of young people delighted themselves.

Upon these bright scenes I now frequently dwell,
  Whilst memory recounts them with feelings of
    pleasure ;
Of them, and of past Sabbath days I will tell,
  When blessings were felt without limit or measure.

All, all are now past, and fresh objects appear,
  Around Oakengates many beauties are seen ;
Yes, some in the distance, and others quite near,
  With woodlands and wide-spreading meadows
    between.

Then adieu to past scenes, no more they may gladden
  Mine eyes and my heart while a sojourner here ;
But parting with them my spirits shall not sadden,
  Nor cause me to sigh, nor to drop e'en a tear.

I'll visit the Wrekin, and from its proud summit,
  Survey the fair country encircling its base ;
With a heart full of gratitude, standing upon it,
  Give vent to my feelings in language of praise.

And oft in the Church that is close by my dwelling,
  I'll speak of God's love in the gifts He has given ;
And pray that each heart with pure love may be
    swelling,
  Until we are raised to sing anthems in heaven.

—:o:—

On Visiting Stratford-on-Avon,

JULY 16TH, 1877.

HAIL STRATFORD! hail! thy suburbs fair,
Present attractions great and rare,
  Peculiarly thine own :
Nature with lavish hand has spread
Beauties around where e'er I tread,
  In country and in town.

The Avon flows through thy domain,
And how profuse the golden grain
  Appears on every hand!
Umbrageous trees enhance the scene,
And flowers of every hue and mien,
  Luxuriant, rich, and grand.

Thy lovely walks and sylvan bowers,
Thy ancient piles and hoary towers,
  And truly classic ground ;
May well attract the stranger's feet,
Afford the thoughtful mind a treat ;
  Sublime, and yet profound.

One of thy sons of world-wide fame,
In thee immortalized his name ;
  And shed a lustre o'er
This nation, which will never wane,
But every age fresh brightness gain,
  Till time shall be no more.

The house where first he saw the light,
Now stands in antiquated plight,
    With curious relics fraught ;
His chair, and writing desk as well,
Of by-past times most clearly tell,
    When SHAKSPEARE lived and wrote.

And in a cot not far away,
There lived a maid called HATHAWAY,
    Whom SHAKSPEARE wooed and won ;
To this, the prying oft resort,
To see where he once paid his court,
    And where her life begun.

The noble Avon gently flows
Close by where multitudes repose
    Beneath the verdant sward :
And in the Church, beneath a stone,
There lies the dust of him who's known
    As England's greatest Bard.

The chancel of the Church contains
The Poet's wife and child's remains,—
    All three lie side by side ;
And tablets rare adorn the place,
True records of a worthy race,—
    Old Stratford's joy and pride.

Hail Stratford ! hail ! thy famous dead,
Around thy history have shed
    A lustre that will last,
When other scenes of great renown,
Have lost their glory and their crown,
    Forgotten in the past.

Clent Hills, Worcestershire.

There are many bright spots
    As we wander through life ;
With beauty and grandeur
    Nature's temple is rife :
Above and around us,
    Divine wisdom is seen—
In the star-spangled heavens,
    And earth's carpet of green.

To gaze on this temple,
    My glad footsteps I bent,
And quickly ascended
    The renown'd hills of Clent ;
From the summit of which,
    This vast temple I view'd,
And for its Great Framer,
    Felt with rev'rence imbued.

The landscape—how charming !
    A panorama grand ;
What woods, streams, and hedges,
    Stretching over the land !
What villas and churches
    From this eminence seen !
All forming a contrast
    To earth's carpet of green.

The park—so extensive—
    Of fair Hagley is near :
Connected with it, are
    Reminiscences dear :

There, THOMSON, whose " *Seasons,*"
　　Immortalis'd his name,
Oft wander'd while musing,
　　And augmented its fame

Sweet voices assail me,
　　Many children are near ;
Some mounted on donkeys,
　　Others walk in the rear :
All happy and joyous,
　　O ! how grotesque the scene ;
While some are reclining
　　On earth's carpet of green.

How rapidly a train
　　I see moving along
E'er rumbling and puffing
　　Rich scenery among :
Disappearing at times,
　　Then emerging again ;
Well freighted with mortals
　　Is that passenger train.

And lo ! now another
　　Just appearing in sight,
Its course indicated
　　By a streamer of white,—
Now rising—then curling,—
　　Ever varying the scene,
As the train passes on,
　　O'er earth's carpet of green.

A bevy of wild-fowl
　　Is approaching the hills ;
And now, just above me,
　　A Lark merrily trills :

But from yonder rook'ry,
　Tuneless voices I hear ;
Continuous cawings,
　Greet harshly mine ear.

O ! yes, many bright spots,
　All enliven'd with mirth,
Oft fall to the lot of
　The denizens of earth ;
Around them sweet songsters,
　And gay flow'rets are seen ;
Enamelled all over
　Is earth's carpet of green.

This beautiful prospect
　Quite entrancing my soul,
Leads me to adore Thee,
　Thou Great Maker of all :
O ! may Thy good Spirit
　Ever to me be given ;
Then take me, O ! take me
　To Thy temple in heaven !

The Brierley Hill Catastrophe.

Descriptive of the thrilling incidents connected with the imprison-
ment of thirteen Miners in Lock's Lane Pit, who were entombed alive
five days and five nights, from March 16th, 1869. Twelve of them
were rescued alive.

HARK ! hark ! a wailing sound is heard,
Lo ! many hearts with grief are stirr'd,
Numerous faces look aghast,
And many tears are falling fast,

A wide-spread panic has begun,
People with perturbation run,
Some scarcely speak above their breath,
And all have sadd'ning thoughts of death.

At Lock's Lane Pit they congregate,
And there discuss the hapless fate
Of men and boys alive entombed
Deep, deep below,—perchance all doomed
To death, but hearts and hands combine
To work their rescue from the mine.

Yes, thirteen precious souls are there,
Wholly shut in from light and air,
Shut in by a gathering flood,
And soon quite destitute of food ;
Five dismal days and nights are pass'd,
O what a long and bitter fast !
Sometimes singing—praying—crying,
With thoughts of home and thoughts of dying.

HICKMAN resolves, while he has breath,
To sing and pray, and thus meet death ;
He bears his family on his mind,
But to his lot is quite resigned.
And HANLEY finds religion sweet,
It makes his soul for glory meet ;
He hopes in God, and hopes to rise
To join his Saviour in the skies.

TAYLOR and HUNT, we trust, in prayer,
Feel happy while imprisoned there.
PAGE knows " in heaven there still is light,"
Though round them reigns perpetual night ;
When HOLDEN feels the chast'ning rod,
PAGE cries, " Keep up your faith in God."

And while they sing, and while they pray,
Young SANKEY sleeps much time away :
Sleep on, poor boy ! and take thy rest,
Thou art not now with grief oppressed.

PEARSON and SON,—brave boy is he !
Sits close beside his father's knee,
Most gladly helping all the while
His father's moments to beguile ;
He talks of dear ones far above,
And feels for them a stronger love ;
He hopes again to kiss his mother,
Also his sister and his brother ;
The father finds that this sweet boy
Is now his comfort and his joy.

Poor HIGGS ! his strength is failing fast,
Forsaken by his mates at last,
Can scarcely crawl along the ground,
Expects to be soon choked or drowned ;
Without a sympathiser near,
He thinks of wife and children dear,
He breathes for them a fervent prayer,
And gives them to Jehovah's care.

Undaunted SKIDMORE nobly gave
His bread young TIMMINS' life to save,
And hugg'd him close to keep him warm,
Himself regardless of all harm.
Well done ! young man, thy kindly heart
Has made affection's tear to start ;
Thy gen'rous deed emblazed shall be :
May heavenly blessings rest on thee.

Young SANKEY too, was kindly fed,
By TAYLOR, for a time, with bread ;
And HUNT his crust most gladly shared,
When all was gone,—they strangely fared,—
Some eating coals,—some chewing leather,
Hung'ring and suff'ring altogether.

Poor ASHMAN'S reason took its flight,
And he became a madman quite ;
He tore his clothes and wildly fled
From all the rest, and soon was dead.

While all in darkness here remain,
Excited thousands crowd Lock's Lane ;
Wives, and mothers, and sisters there,
With haggard looks,—dishevelled hair,
And scalding tears bedew each cheek,
Far more is felt than tongue can speak ;
Alternate hopes and fears arise,
While friends and strangers sympathise,
And many pray that God would save
The loved ones from a living grave.

See, hour by hour,—both night and day,
Men pump to draw the flood away;
And some descend,—heroic men !
But choke-damp drives them back again :
Again, again, quite down the shaft
They go,—and with a floating raft ;
Success attends their efforts then,
Each time returning with lost men :
Loud peans make the welkin ring
As to the top these men they bring ;

Cheer after cheer ascends for BROWN,
For PLANT and THOMPSON, who went down,
Risking their lives these men to save
From death and from a watery grave.
Philanthropists! Courageous band!!
Your fame shall spread throughout the land;
Your names inscribed on history's page,
Be handed down from age to age.

The wife and mother, filled with joy,
Now clasps her husband and her boy;
The sister hugs her darling brother,
Frantic with joy they greet each other;
The suff'rers soon in fresh attire,
Are gently placed beside the fire,
Warm milk and stimulants are given,
And many thanks sent up to heaven;
Suspense, and fear, and grief are past,
The lost ones are restored at last.

On Sabbath let the house of God,
Devoutly by your feet be trod,
And there let all unite to raise
A song of heartfelt, grateful praise,
For this deliverance from the Mine,
Each cry, O Lord, I will be thine.

To a more dreadful pit than this,
Exposed each godless sinner is,
And from it Christ alone can save,
For us His precious life He gave;
Then fly to Him while mercy's given,
And find, through Him, your way to heaven.

RELIGIOUS.

—:o:—

Heaven.

———

A LITTLE BOY lay on his bed,
  Near eight years old was he ;
With pain his tender frame and head
Were rack'd, but to his mother said,
  " Mamma, now talk with me."

" What shall I talk about, my dear?
  My heart with grief is riven ; "
This made him strive her heart to cheer,
And said, " Mamma, come very near,
  And let us talk of heaven."

" Tell me of Jesus Christ," he said,
  " To love Him well I've striven
Through days and nights upon this bed,
And soon I hope to rest my head
  Upon His breast in heaven."

" Tell me of angels bright and fair,
  To whom gold crowns are given :
Tell me of saints already there ;
O, how I long their joys to share,
  And dwell with them in heaven."

" Tell me, Mamma, of heavenly songs,
    Sung in that far-off haven ;
Where storms and dangers, griefs and wrongs,
Are quite unknown to happy throngs
    Of blood-wash'd souls in heaven."

" And tell me too, of children fair,
    About the age of seven,
Whom I shall have for comrades, where
We'll taste of pleasures pure and rare,—
    For such are found in heaven."

" Tell me about their shining dress,—
    As white as snow just driven ;
Of harps and palms which all possess,
Also of endless happiness,
    In that sweet land of heaven."

" Farewell ! Mamma,—adieu all pain,—
    A long respite is given ;
I go with Jesus Christ to reign,
For me to die is untold gain : "
    He died—and entered heaven.

Humility.

THE LARK soars aloft, and charmingly sings,
At earliest morn with dew on his wings ;
Not caring to wait for a wond'ring throng
To admire his flight, and applaud his song.

But though he's so high, and seems but a dot,
His nest he has placed on a lowly spot ;
Not caring to build on a lofty tower,—
On a tree or shrub in the garden bower.

The Nightingale too delightfully sings,
And oft with his music the welkin rings ;
Choosing the thickets to warble among,
The darker the night, the sweeter his song.

He heeds not the praise of those whom he charms,
As sweetly he trills, quite free from alarms ;
His symphonies swelling and rising the higher,
Yet never appearing to falter or tire.

The Violet small and beautiful too,
Grows best in the shade, as if hiding from view ;
Its stalk gently curved, its head hanging low,
Apparently shunning the sun's burning glow.

What flower can with its great beauty compare,
Or shed such delicious perfume on the air ?
In places remote performing its part,—
Delighting the eye, and gladd'ning the heart.

Lov'd emblems are these of the Christian here,
Contented he lives in this changing sphere ;
In brightness or gloom he's always the same,—
If godly in heart, as well as in name.

Retiring and humble in mind and in life,
Eschewing earth's honours, and riches, and strife ;
He aims not at anything worldly and great,
But satisfied quite in a lowly estate.

Undying Things.

Tune,—"Kind Words can Never Die."

————

PURE love can never die,
    Clear as noonday;
    Knowledge will by and bye
    Vanish away;
Yea, tongues shall ever cease,
And fail shall prophecies,
But love, in realms of peace,
    Shall live for aye.
Pure love can never die, never die, &c.

    Good deeds can never die,
    Aye, live they must,
    Though in the grave we lie
    Crumbling to dust;
Our deeds if good and true,
Will live and minds imbue,
Not like the morning dew
    Soon pass away.
Good deeds can never die, never die, &c.

    God's word can never die,
    'Tis like Himself;
    Earth's fame and joys will fly,
    And sordid pelf;
How soon they disappear,
All, all is transient here,
Death and the grave are near,
    We pass away;
God's word can never die, never die, &c.

Souls, souls can never die,
In bliss or pain ;
If pure will mount on high
With Christ to reign ;
Our frames will waste away,
Though sprightly, young, and gay,
But souls with Jesus may
In glory live,
Souls, souls can never die, never die, &c.

Heaven's joys can never die,
Full, fresh, and clear ;
There angels never sigh,
Nor shed a tear ;
Supernal glory reigns
O'er all the heavenly plains,
There too immortal strains
Roll, roll along,
Heaven's joy can never die, never die, &c.

" We all do Fade as a Leaf."

ISAIAH LXIV. 6.

" WE all do fade as a leaf,"
Cried the prophet in days of old ;
Man's earthly sojourn is brief,
'Tis just like "a tale that is told."

" We all do fade as a leaf,"
Our days few, and stricken with woe :
Our path is sadden'd with grief,
While treading this region below.

" We all do fade as a leaf,"
  And like it shall speedily fall;
Here all is transcient and brief,—
  How solemn the lesson to all !

" We all do fade as a leaf,"
  By death of our vigour be shorn;
He'll come, perchance, like a thief
  At midnight, or else in the morn.

" We all do fade as a leaf,"
  Like it—by the wind chas'd away,—
We'll pass from this world of grief,
  No more in this region to stay.

" We all do fade as a leaf,"
  Our bodies like it shall decay:
To sainted souls a relief,
  Which ascend to the realms of day.

" We all do fade as a leaf,"
  Let man then for heaven prepare:
Let this be his business chief,
  That he may land happily there.

There, leaves ne'er wither nor fade,
  But wear a perennial hue;
Sunshine without any shade,
  And flow'rets ne'er moisten'd with dew.

There, bowers of amaranth bloom,
  And trees bear ambrosial fruit;
Angels are strangers to gloom,
  Ever tuning the heavenly lute.

Pastures in immortal green,
  And water as clear as the light,
Are bath'd in celestial sheen,
  And never enshrouded in night.

" Eye hath not seen " its bright plains,
  Its citizens beauteous and fair;
" Ear hath not heard " their sweet strains,
  Nor shall we, till safe landed there.

" Heart can't conceive " the vast bliss
  Prepar'd for the righteous above;
Pure and exalted it is,
  And proves that Jehovah is love.

Then leaves may wither and fall,
  And friends and relations depart;
Earth's griefs the heart may appal,
  And cause human nature to smart:

But heaven's an unchanging sphere,
  Affording unbounded delight;
If man but lives for it here,
  He'll pass to yon kingdom of light.

Welcome to Christmas.

CHRISTMAS, we welcome thy return,—
  Though very chill thy breath may be,
  And though thy hoary garb we see,
Gladly to thee our thoughts we turn.

Thou com'st with tidings ever glad,
  Tidings of life, and joy, and peace,
  Of ONE who makes our strifes to cease,
Who heals the sick, and cheers the sad.

At thy first advent angels sang,
  And glory burst from heaven on earth,
  To celebrate the Saviour's birth,
And heaven's high courts with music rang.

" Glory to God,"—o'er Bethlehem's plain,
  Sounded from voices in the air,
  " Goodwill to all men " everywhere,
For Jesus shall o'er all men reign.

Jesus is the King of kings,
  He lives, though on the Cross was slain ;
  Though buried too, He rose again,
Yes, rose with healing in His wings.

Lo ! on His head are many crowns,
  O'er earthly potentates He reigns,
  And universal sway maintains,
For all in earth and heaven He owns.

His reign will be continued ever,
  His glory last through endless day,
  And though assailed His kingdom may,
Destroyed His kingdom shall be never.

Then, Christmas, thou art welcome here,
  Thy coming fills our hearts with glee,
  Our Advent songs refer to thee,
For all rejoice when thou art near.

FAMILY REMINISCENCES.

—o—

In Memory of my dear Wife,

WHO DIED IN CHRIST, AT PICKERING, YORKSHIRE, AUG. 30 1859.

How hard it is, as one by one,
　Our dearest friends depart ;
To say, " O Lord, Thy will be done,"
　And feel it in the heart.

When mother died,—how keen the stroke !
　I felt it much and long ;
And father's sudden death awoke,
　Emotions deep and strong.

Two sisters and a brother dear,
　In distant graveyards sleep ;
For them spontaneous dropp'd the tear,
　Ah ! who could help but weep ?

But now, a heavier stroke's been given,
　My well-beloved is gone ;
She's passed away from earth to heaven,—
　She's now a shining one.

Shining with splendour brighter far,
　Than crowns of earthly gold ;
Yea, brighter than the brightest star
　Which human eyes behold.

Amidst angelic hosts she moves,
  More glorious than the sun ;
The Lamb adoring, whom she loves,—
  Through whom she vict'ry won.

I almost think I hear her sing,
  And harp the heavenly lays ;
Th' eternal hills with music ring,
  For saints unnumber'd praise.

They sing to HIM whose precious blood,
  On Calv'ry's cross was spilt,
To make us kings and priests to God,
  And wash away our guilt.

My lov'd-one often cheer'd my heart,
  And drove my cares away ;
Her gentle kindness did impart
  Fresh pleasures day by day.

In her maternal feelings glow'd,
  And beautified her life ;
Her tender words and actions show'd
  The ever duteous wife.

But while she lov'd her fam'ly dear,
  She lov'd her Saviour too :
And said she felt HIM sweetly near,
  When death was just in view.

Death had no sting—the grave no dread,
  Her mind was calm and even ;
Resign'd her charge, and softly said,
  " We'll meet again in heaven."

A mother's loss,—ah ! who can tell ?
  My children know it not :
But this to feel and know full well,
  Is now my painful lot.

And shall I murmur? No, I'll say,
" Thy will, my God, be done,"
May I for more submission pray,
And reach at last Thy throne.

Raise me and mine to her we love,
In mansions bright and fair ;
Raise us to sing with saints above,—
O that we all were there.

There—there to dwell, and never die,
And nought our union sever,
For HE who reigns enthroned on high,
Will knit our souls for ever.

On the Death of my dear Sister, Mrs. Norman,

WHO SWEETLY FELL ASLEEP IN JESUS, AUGUST 13TH, 1851.

A WELL-BELOVED sister has just past away,
To dwell in the regions of unending day !
The tenement alone rest under the sod,
The tenant has happily gone up to God.

To mourn her departure,—how foolish 'twould be,
Since she is from sorrow for ever set free ;
Pain, sickness, and death, she no more will endure,
For life everlasting to her is secure.

She now treads the plains of yon heavenly land,
And mingles sweet strains with its rapturous band ;
Her lyre symphonious with cadences sweet,
And her happiness is for ever complete.

What grandeur! what glory! encircle her brow;
What myriads of angels encompass her now!
How spotless her raiment! how dazzling her crown,
Which she has, through Jesus, obtained as her own.

Her present abode,—how different from this!
While here she had sorrow,—but now she has bliss;
While here she was tempted, afflicted, and tried,
But for ever now safe by her Saviour's side.

O blessed transition! O glorious change!
To leave scenes terrestrial heaven's kingdom to range;
To fly like a bird that's escap'd from the snare,
And mounts on glad pinions far up in the air.

How unspeakably grand to follow her flight,
And join her again in yon mansions of light!
In glory transcendent for ever to reign,
And never to part from my sister again.

Lines on Visiting my Native Place,

MIDDLETON-IN-TEESDALE, SEPTEMBER 13, 1859.

PECULIARLY dear is the place of one's birth,
Is any place else half so dear upon earth?
Just one,—'tis the place where Christ's spiritual reign
Begins in the heart, and the soul's born again.

The former—nought, nought from the mind can efface,
No circumstance change one's regard for the place;
It's name is held sacred—it's history scann'd,
It's environs regarded as some fairyland;
It's people respected as noble and true,
Their faults and their failings considered as few;
Their houses and gardens, their shops and their trade,
Are view'd with deep interest of every grade.

Inspired with emotions and feelings like these,
I visited lately the banks of the Tees ;
And onward to Middleton wended my way,
To look at the scenes of my juvenile play.

A period of thirty-one years had rolled o'er,
Since I had beheld the lov'd village before ;
The people were changed,—but I thought I'd enquire
How many were there who remembered my sire.
Vast numbers had fallen a prey to the grave,
The young and the old, and the timid and brave :
But a dear quondam friend I met in the way,
With whom on the village-green oft I did play ;
And delighted we were once more to resort
To the neighb'ring scenes of our juvenile sport ;
With feelings of pleasure the past we review'd,
And childhood's bright morning again seemed renew'd.

O, childhood ! bright childhood ! and scenes of my youth !
When innocence, virtue, affection, and truth,
Illumin'd my path, and encircl'd my brow,
How gladly I'd welcome ye back to me now !
But ah ! ye are past—the bright vision is o'er,
Your sunshine and pleasure I'll witness no more.

Middleton ! again I must bid thee farewell,
Within thy fair suburbs I gladly would dwell ;
But when at a distance, nought, nought shall erase
My rev'rence and love for the people and place.

On Visiting the Graves of my Parents,

AT WIGTON, CUMBERLAND, JUNE 18, 1865.

—

How solemn and sacred the ground
　　Where lie the remains of the dead !
We rev'rently gaze on each mound,
　　As silently round them we tread.

Ah ! how many mourners have stood,
　　And wept by the side of the grave—
Of the profligate and of the good,
　　The timid and also the brave ?

And can I unmoved view the tombs
　　Wherein my loved parents now sleep?
Ah ! no, over me there now comes
　　A feeling that moves me to weep.

How precious to me is their dust !
　　More precious than silver or gold ;
And to their dear mem'ry I must
　　Their numerous virtues unfold.

They constantly sought to imbue
　　The minds of their children with truth ;
And greatly rejoic'd as they grew
　　In wisdom through childhood and youth.

Their counsels,—how tender and wise !
    And often most solemnly given ;
O may we their efforts still prize,
    And follow their footsteps to heaven !

The pious example they set,
    Is deeply impress'd on the heart ;
How can we such goodness forget,
    Or from their instructions depart ?

Nor can we forget how we bow'd
    At the family altar each day,
And there heard our dear sire aloud
    For blessings most earnestly pray.

Farewell, honoured parents, farewell !
    The pathway to glory you trod ;
And now in that region you dwell,
    Ascribing loud praises to God.

We'll meet you again by and bye,
    And join in the praise of His name ;
The joys of that land never die,
    Your bliss is for ever the same.

In Loving Remembrance of my Nephew,

JAMES HENDERSON WHITE, WHO WAS DROWNED WHILST BATHING,
AT NEWPORT, MONMOUTHSHIRE, SEPTEMBER 13TH, 1866,
AGED EIGHT YEARS.

FAREWELL, my boy,—my darling boy,
    We miss thy smiling face ;
Thou wert thy parents' hope and joy,
    But brief has been thy race.

Sprightly, intelligent, and kind,
    A healthy, happy boy ;
From day to day thou seem'st to find
    Pure bliss without alloy.

Can we forget thy sportive ways
    When we saw thee rejoice ?
Ah ! no, we now recall those days,
    And think we hear thy voice.

Thy merry laugh,—thy cheerful song,—
    Thy shouts of youthful glee :
To think of these can not be wrong,—
    We love to think of thee.

Those gladsome, playful days are o'er,
    Thy friends now mourn for thee :
Death came in an unlooked for hour,
    And set thy spirit free.

Freed from the tenement of clay,
    It rose with God to dwell,
To spend a bright, unending day,
    Where heavenly anthems swell.

Thy voice melodious here below,
    Is tuned to songs divine ;
And now in praise and rapt'rous awe,
    With angel-hosts combine.

May we, who mourn for thee, my boy,
    No longer sadly grieve ;
But haste to share thy untold joy,
    In endless bliss to live.

In Loving Memory of my dear Nephew,

William M. Sutton, of Carlisle, who fell asleep in Jesus,

November 11th, 1883; Aged 27 Years.

————

Ah! cruel Death, again thy venomed dart
Has pierced a youthful, loving heart !
Another victim fills a grave,—
Another whom no skill could save.

Beside his couch, as there he lay,
Some loving ones watched night and day,
Striving the sufferers mind to cheer,
Because to them he was most dear.

With gentle hand and tender heart,
They strove true comfort to impart :
But nought could save the vital flame,
Nought could avert Death's certain aim.

True piety was there, and shone
With lustre in the suffering one ;
Yes, meekness, love, and patience rare,—
Combined with faith and fervent prayer.

And in the past he oft had stood,
To speak of Christ's most precious blood ;
Pointing to young and old the way
Which leads to everlasting day.

How often too, with tuneful voice,
He made the hearts of all rejoice ;
Singing the praises of the LAMB,—
The SPIRIT, and the great I AM.

But now, his voice is no more heard,
By it no Christian hearts are stirred :
It mingles with the hosts above,
Who sing of Christ's redeeming love.

To him a glorious crown is given,
A robe, and palm, and harp in heaven,
And there amid the angel-choir,
He helps to swell the anthem higher !

Euthanasia :

A SONNET IN MEMORY OF MY DEAR BROTHER, THOMAS WHITE,
LATE OF RIPON, WHO PASSED PEACEFULLY AWAY TO HIS
ETERNAL REST, JUNE 10TH, 1880, AGED 74 YEARS.

My dearly-loved brother is gone,—
A crown and a kingdom he's won,
And heard the grand plaudit, "Well done,"
　　For faithfully serving his God :
His life, O how usefully spent !
On doing good always intent,—
To the sick and the dying he went,
　　And thus in Christ's footsteps he trod.
A writer—a preacher—a bard,
'Gainst Satan and error he warr'd,
And now he receives his reward,
　　Through the merits of Jesus' blood ;
His glory and bliss, who can tell ?
Till we meet,—dear brother,—farewell !

VARIOUS.

—:o:—

On Re-bisiting Keswick, Cumberland,

IN AUGUST, 1869.

———

O, CHARMING spot! I love thee still,
  Scene of my boyish plays ;
Each mountain, valley, lake, and hill,
  Reminds me of those days,—
For which I sigh,—but sigh in vain,
I cannot bring them back again.

What changes in the dear old town !
  It scarcely seems the same ;
In size and population grown,
  Also in wealth and fame ;
Some ancient piles it still retains,—
The old Moot Hall unchanged remains.

And there too, stands my early home,
  Where all the family dwelt ;
And daily, 'neath its honour'd dome,
  We all devoutly knelt,—
While for us our dear aged sire,
Invoked the blessings all require.

Of objects missing, as I turn
  To look for things of yore,
The School House, where I sat to learn
  The elements of lore,
Is one,—it once adorned the town,
But, ah ! rude hands have pulled it down.

The parish Church, still dear, I trust,
    To thousands, greets mine eyes ;
And there the venerated dust
    Of poet SOUTHEY lies ;
Hail! honoured shrine! How oft I've seen
His stately walk and thoughtful mien.

Once to the Poet's house I went,
    A servant took my card,
Which to her lord she did present,
    And this brought out the Bard ;
Who smiled, and spoke so kindly then,
I thought he was the best of men.

That dwelling place once more I spy,
    A picturesque retreat !
The river Greta flows close by,
    With bubbling music sweet ;
On its banks the laureate mused,
And classic authors there perused.

Majestic Skiddaw bounds the view,
    Behind this mansion fair ;
In front are lakes, and meadows too,
    And mountains everywhere ;
And, lo ! a railway train is seen
Gliding these hills and lakes between.

Sweet Derwent vale ! thy scenery grand,
    Is precious to me now ;
No other part of this fair land,
    Is half so fair as thou ;
When distant, still I'll feel thy spell,
Sweet Derwent vale,—farewell ! farewell ! !

On Visiting Bronwylva,

THE RESIDENCE OF THE LATE MRS. HEMANS, AUGUST 22ND, 1867.

How charming the scenery around,
  As viewed from this sylvan retreat!
Where HEMANS, so justly renowned,
  The muses did frequently meet.

Yon mountains in majesty stand,
  O'erlooking the valley below,
Are objects romantic and grand,
  And strike the beholder with awe!

St. Asaph's Cathedral is near,
  A noble and time-honour'd pile!
To true Christian hearts ever dear,
  Where HEMANS resorted awhile.

This mansion,—these gardens and bowers,
  This beautiful lawn and green sward ;
These elegant trees, shrubs, and flowers,
  Have witness'd the walks of the bard.

Her sanctified genius has shed
  A lustre far brighter than gold,—
Which shines—and will shine, though she's dead,
  All over the scenes I behold.

Dear saint ! thou hast since pass'd away,
  Through "The Better Land's" beauties to roam :
While here, t'was the theme of thy lay,
  But now 'tis for ever thy home.

An Elegy

On Visiting the Grave of the Thirty-Three Victims Who Perished on the Railway, near Abergele, August 20th, 1868.

LIGHTLY—solemnly—reverently tread
Amid the remains of the num'rous dead ;
The young, middle-aged, and the old lie here,
Quite equal are now the peasant and peer ;
Howe'er they have lived, they rest here at last,
Each sculptured stone tells a tale of the past,
Recording in brief the name and the age
Of those who have finished life's pilgrimage :
But ah ; how varied these records appear,
Inciting surprise, a sigh, or a tear !
Reminding us all how short is our stay
On earth, we're passing—fast passing away !

Lo ! one tomb of huge dimensions I see,
Containing the dust of thirty and three,
Who quickly perished 'midst devouring flame,
Effacing distinctions of sex, rank, and name ;
The baronet, judge, the stoker, and guard,
Fell victims alike,—their bones were all charred ;
The peer and valet, the lady and maid,
Now mingle, for here their ashes are laid ;
Yes, one common death, and one common grave,
Befel thirty-three whom nothing could save.

The morning was bright, and all hearts were light,
As the train rush'd on with impetuous might,—
Now rumbling along by the ocean's side,
Then rapidly through a deep cutting glide ;
Seen here,—now there,—ah ! in a moment gone,
Whistling, hissing, and puffing anon ;

Many stations were passed with light'ning speed,
For the train was drawn by a fiery steed ;
Some passengers read,—others gaily talk'd,
Some loung'd and slept,—others quaff'd and smok'd,
Their hearts were glad as they thought of each friend
Whom they hop'd to greet at their journey's end.

But Death was near, and he claimed as his prey
A portion of those on that iron way :
Lo ! the vanguard part became wrapt in fire,
And hurried them all to destruction dire ;
The driver, brave man ! took a perilous leap,
And gained in safety the adjacent steep ;
" Jump for your life, Joe," he cried to his mate,
Who, failing, met with a terrible fate ;
While those in the rear all speedily fled
From the burning train, and the burning dead ;
For no human power these victims could save,
They had the same death, and now the same grave.

Around this sepulchre mourners have stood,
Including the plebeian, noble and good ;
All through this charnel-house weeping was heard,
Gazers were silent,—the children scarce stirr'd,
For sad was each heart,—quite stricken with woe,
While all that remained of the dead were laid low,
And " ashes to ashes, and dust to dust,"
Reminded the living that die they must,—
Life is uncertain, and brief is our stay
On earth,—we're passing—fast passing away !

This train is an emblem of man's swift course,
Who no sooner breathes than a secret force
Impels him on, and he passes away
Like an eagle hastening on to its prey,*
Or a post,* or a ship,* that's instantly gone,
E'en so is man's life—passing—passing anon ;

---

*Job ix. 25, 26.

But suddenly Death oft stands in the way,
And seizes alike the grave and the gay ;
His grasp is severe, oft mingled with fire,
And potent indeed is the force of his ire ;
Let man then be wise, and prepare for his end,
Making heaven his aim, and Jesus his friend.

The Rivulet.
(Written in 1840).

FLOW on, flow on, thou sparkling brook,
  (While gentle breezes blow),
Around the rocks and sheltered nook,
  And through the fields below,
Where cattle bask upon thy brink,
And of thy limpid waters drink.

Upon thy banks I love to sit,
  And view their motley vest ;
I love to cull the violet,
  Out from among the rest
Of scented flowers, which deck thy brim,
And hear each feather'd songster's hymn.

Thy bubbling sound I love to hear,
  And view thy pebbly bed,
Which sparkles through thy stream so clear,
  When Sol's bright rays are shed :
At eventide I love to view
Within thy stream the moon's pale hue.

Then still flow on, thou murm'ring rill,
  While Summer's beauties shine :
And may thy mystic music still
  Salute these ears of mine,
Until I quit this vale of tears,
And heavenly sounds salute mine ears.

To the Violet.

(Written in 1841.)

———

PRETTY flower of humble mien,
In the woods and meadows seen,
Also on the mountain's side,
Where the gentle zephyrs glide ;
And beside the rivulet,
Thou dost grow, my violet.

Lilies, king-cups, cowslips, all,
Though thou art so very small,
Wears a richer coat than they,
Thou art prettier far away ;
Not one flower have I seen yet,
Sweet as thee, my violet.

Buttercups and daisies too,
Ope their leaves to greet our view ;
But their hues are not so meet,
Nor their odours half so sweet
To my taste, since first I met
Thee, my pretty violet.

For the foxglove's gaudy hue,
I would not give thee in lieu ;
Thou art lovelier by far,
For thy tints much sweeter are ;
Not one flower have I seen yet,
Pretty as my violet.

Nor within the garden bower,
Can I find so sweet a flower;
There the blushing rose is seen,
Tulips too of lofty mien;
But not one have I seen yet,
Lovely as my violet.

Then I'll plant thee near my cot,
Thou shalt have a favoured spot;
There thy fragrance shed around,
Let thy rich perfume abound,
For no flower have I seen yet,
Charming as my violet.

The Lake District, Cumberland: A Sonnet.

On every side high mountains stand,
  And some with features wild and grand ;
Majestic rocks enhance the scene,
With strips of grass, quite fresh and green,
Appearing here and there between,—
  As if produced by magic wand.
Gigantic Skiddaw seems to frown,
From his proud altitude looks down,
  Surveying distant seas and land.
The placid lakes with beauty rife,
Far, far away from din and strife,
Bear on their bosoms signs of life :
  And in the valleys all around,
  Plenty, and peace, and joy abound.

The Orphan Boy: A Tale.

(Written in 1840).

———

At night, quite sad, upon a stone
I saw him sitting all alone ;
No friend was nigh to soothe his grief,
Or to his wants impart relief.

Approaching him, I said, " my lad,
" What makes you look so very sad ?
" Why shed those bitter tears and moan?
" Arise, and quickly leave this stone."

A timid glance, as there he sat,
He gave,—his heart went pit-a-pat ;
His clothes all tattered,—visage wan,—
He thus his mournful tale began :—

" Kind Sir, pray hear, I have no home,
" I am quite left at large to roam,
" Without a single friend on earth,
" Not even those who gave me birth.

" My mother died when I was born,
" And left me nearly quite forlorn ;
" Except my father's watchful care,
" Who for me offer'd fervent prayer.

" He train'd me in the way to heaven,
" Till I was just turn'd aged seven ;
" And then he too was call'd away,
" To join her in bright realms of day.

" Brothers and sisters I have none,
" Into a better world they're gone;
" Their bodies rest beneath the sod,
" Their souls have wing'd their way to God."

When thus he'd spoke, he faintly sigh'd,
He groan'd, fell back, and there he died;
His soul escap'd to realms of bliss,
To join them all where Jesus is.

I thought how thankful I should be,
That I'm not destitute like he;
That I so richly do enjoy
More blessings than the Orphan Boy.

The Farmer's Blunder.

A WORTHY Rustic and his wife,
    Lived on a little farm;
Their prospects brighten'd all through life,
    'Twas seldom they took harm.

One Winter, sure enough, at last,
    Misfortune them befel;
The snow had fallen thick and fast,
    And lay in drifts as well.

They had a barn, so old and frail,
    That some said, " By-and-bye,
Beneath the weight of snow 'twill fail,
    And all in ruins lie."

The Farmer, doubtless, thought the same,
  For he was wide awake;
And so, before the next snow came,
  He did precaution take.

He gave his spouse to understand,
  His fixed resolve to go
And mount the barn, with spade in hand,
  To shovel off the snow.

He tied a rope end round his waist,
  The other round his wife;
And then to work he made all haste,
  As if for very life.

The snow, *en masse*, did sudd'nly slide,
  The worthy Farmer too ;
And as he dropp'd down on one side,
  His wife he upward drew.

So on one side the Farmer hung,
  And loud for help did cry;
Whilst on the other his wife was slung,
  Both dangling high and dry.

The Farmer could not help his wife
  She could not help her man ;
At length, a neighbour, with a knife,
  To free them quickly ran.

He cut the rope, and down they fell,
  But were not hurt,—a wonder ;
And oft the people laugh and tell
  About the Farmer's blunder.

The Chimney Sweep and the Thieves.

A FARMER, who liv'd far away
In the country, wanted a sweep ;
So drove to the town one fine day,
For a boy up chimneys to creep.

Such a boy was found, but, alas !
He could not ride there in his soot ;
For sure he belonged to a class,
Whose garments another would smut.

The journey, however, he took,
Arriving sometime in the night ;
And found in the barn a snug nook,
To rest till the next morning light.

He had not been there very long,
When two men drove up with a hack ;
They entered the barn, (O how wrong !)
And with grain fill'd sack after sack.

" A third person should have been here,
To hold us the candle," one said ;
Not knowing that one was so near,
Who only had just gone to bed.

Quite snugly ensconced among sheaves,
Poor Sooty, though taking his rest,
Not dreaming the men were two thieves,
Was willing to help them his best.

" O, I'll hold the candle," he said,
   And straightway he ran to the place ;
But fright seized the thieves,—and they fled,
   As soon as they saw his black face.

They thought he had come from below,
   To help them to do what was evil ;
So hack, sacks, and all they forego,
   Declining to work with the devil.

Poor Sooty stood looking amazed,
   When he saw how wildly they fled ;
And after them sometime he gazed,
   Then wisely return'd to his bed.

" The wicked, how quickly they flee,
   When no man pursueth,"* said one ;
The statement is true as we see,
   They're stricken with terror,—*and gone !*

The Deaf and Dumb Child.

A LITTLE girl, born deaf and dumb,
   But very bright and cute;
Was ask'd one day, if she could tell
   Why she was born a mute.
She smiled and wept, then quickly wrote
   An answer just and right,—
'Twas this,—" E'en so, Father, for so
   It seem'd good in thy sight."†

---

* PROVERBS xxviii. 1 v.   † ST. MATTHEW xi. 26 v.

The Student and the Labourer.

A LEARNED Professor was taking his walk,
A Student was with him, with whom he did talk ;
They wander'd through meadows where rivulets glide,
Enjoying the calm of the sweet eventide.

The cattle were lowing close by the field-gate,
A Rustic was ploughing apart from his mate,—
Who, barefooted, plodded his wearisome way,
Bemoaning in silence his niggardly pay.

His shoes, to last longer, were put on one side,
And though feeling languid, he earnestly plied
Himself to his labour, which soon he would leave,
For round him were closing the shadows of eve.

The Student, with glee, said, " These shoes I will hide,
And what fun it will be to skulk on one side,
Watching the poor fellow's sad look of despair,
As he wanders and seeks for them here and there."

The Professor replied, " That never will do,
'Twould be better to place a coin in each shoe ;
Then witness the poor man's surprise and delight,
To find, unexpected, a treasure so bright."

The Student consented, and put in each shoe,
A very bright dollar, quite sparkling and new ;
Then fled from the spot behind bushes to hide,
And watch'd, till the man leaving work, he espied.

The Labourer put his right foot in his shoe,
But felt something hard, and his foot he withdrew ;
Then stooping, he look'd in, and saw with surprise,
A something which gladdened his heart and his eyes.

His left foot he next ventured softly to place
In the other, when, lo! was seen in his face
Amazement and joy, while his foot he withdrew,
For another bright coin was found in that shoe.

He fell on his knees, and with uplifted hands,
Offered thanks unto God, who owns seas and lands,
For this timely help when afflictions were sore,
And starvation had entered his cottage door.

The Student now saw that the deed he had done,
Was better by far than the coveted fun;
And firmly that Scripture he now did believe,
" 'Tis more blessed to give, than 'tis to receive."

A Good Wife.

(A RESEMBLANCE AND A DIFFERENCE.)

JUST like three things, a wife should be,
 Yet these should not resemble;
'Tis strange but true, as you shall see,
 For I will not dissemble.

First, like a good Town-Clock, keep time,
 And orderly appear;
But never, like it, speak so loud
 That all the town may hear.

Next, like a Snail, a wife should keep
 At home, in duty's track;
But never, like a Snail, should she
 Take all upon her back.

And, lastly, like an Echo true,—
 Speak when she's spoken to:
But not resolved, like it, to have
 The last word after you.

A Fickle Swain.

A CERTAIN Swain oft fell in love,
 But never yet was able
To continue his amours long
 For he was quite unstable.

A lovely maid in youthful prime,
 First gained his fickle heart;
Amye, her name—and oft he vowed
 From her he'd never part.

But, by-and-bye, sweet *Floriat* came,
 To lure him with her charms,
Who soon was in her rival's place,
 And taken to his arms.

A few months pass'd, and then he saw,
 A pretty maiden, very;
Cynthia's form was beautiful,
 Her mind was light and merry.

Amoroso could not long resist
 The influence of this charmer:
He woo'd—he won—and felt his heart
 Towards her becoming warmer.

A little time pass'd on, and then
 Fair *Phillis* met his view,
Who seemed to have—at least to him—
 Attractions great and new.

All former *belles* were now forgot,
 For she absorbed his heart,
Until a prettier maid than she,
 Made him with wonder start.

Clorris had such bewitching eyes,
  Such lovely hands and feet;
Such rosy cheeks, and ruby lips,—
  To see them was a treat.

O, how he long'd to make her his!
  He called her " Pet" and " Dove ;"
Surpassing all he'd seen before,
  No other could he love.

But *Amaryllis* next appeared,
  And smote him with her charms;
He then resolved to win her heart,
  And clasp her in his arms.

This soon he did,—and oft he thought
  She was almost divine,—
He said, " How happy I shall be
  When I can call her mine.

But, lo! another cross'd his path,
  She was an angel quite;
So comely, tall, and elegant,—
  Her dress, too, neat and light.

Her name was *Blanche*, a *belle* indeed,
  So ladylike and nice;
To her he paid his court in terms,
  Quite measured and precise.

But here, he failed to gain his suit,
  She scorn'd it, and repell'd him;
And soon on other lady's tracks,—
  His friends, amused, beheld him.

In short, this fickle Swain could not
  Go unconcernedly past
A lady fair,—for he lov'd best
  The one he saw the last.

Penelope's web, his heart was like,
    Yes, changing—changing ever;
His mind was like the weathercock,
    And to be trusted *never.*

The Kite:
Or, Pride must have a Fall.

It happen'd one beautiful Summer day,
I noticed some frolicsome boys at play:
And one, with a string, was holding a kite,
Which had gained a wondrous and dizzy height.

It appeared to aim at kissing a cloud,
With its great altitude mightily proud;
Not deigning to look on mortals below;
In a world so blighted by sin, death, and woe.

He nodded his head, and he wagged his tail,
As if nothing could now his honour assail;
And he seem'd to say, " What a monarch I am !
" All others below me are fools and a sham.

" Up here, 'tis always as bright as the noon,
" I associate with the sun and the moon;
" At night, the stars will my company keep,
" While mortals beneath are buried in sleep."

He floated along, elated with pride,
Well pleased with his sphere—exalted and wide;
When, lo! the string snapp'd, and down came the Kite,
All tattered and broke, in ignoble plight.

So Pride often causes some men to look down
On others with scorn, and oft with a frown;
They fancy themselves far higher than all,
But soon the string breaks, and Pride has a fall.

On Visiting Paris in 1878.

O CITY of beauty, of fashion, of pleasure !
　How gladly I gaze upon thee ;
Being free from all care, I come at my leisure,
With thousands of Britons, to see thy vast treasure,
　Attractive to them and to me.

Thy history full of dark deeds oft appals,
　And causes the reader to start ;
But, ah ! this fair prospect my spirit enthrals,
Whilst memory some reminiscence recalls,
　Which deeply impresses my heart.

Ah ! who—who could think of a massacre here,
　Forsooth on Bartholomew's day ?
That a horrible death to many was near
In a city so fair and region so clear,
　'Mid scenes of a terrible fray.

The blood of some thousands was wantonly shed,
　And thy streets were cover'd with slain ;
Whilst all loyal hearts were o'erwhelmed with dread,
And bitter and loud were the cries for the dead,
　Which rose from hearts stricken with pain.

Again, and again too, in more recent times,
　The demon of bigoted-hate
Has filled with anguish all countries and climes,
And oft in thy midst has incited to crimes
　Too ghastly for me to relate.

The Germans of late have encompass'd thee round,
  Inflicting great misery and want ;
Their military prowess and skill had no bound,
Thy armies were conquered upon their own ground,
  The enemy no quarter would grant.

And lastly, the Commune, with bloodthirsty zeal,
  Caused anarchy rampant to reign ;
For those who were helpless no pity could feel,
And made all thy peaceable citizens reel
  With anguish, and horor, and pain.

Thy noble Tuileries a ruin now stands,
  A spectacle of Communal hate ;
Walls blackened and roofless, the work of wild bands,
Who first on its treasures laid violent hands ;
  How terribly sad is its fate !

But now, all is peace and prosperity here,
  Thy people industrious and free;
They now can dwell safely, without any fear,
The fruits of the Great Exhibition appear;
  All nations now flock into thee.

How lively and gay are thy Boulevards now!
  On river and rail there is life ;
To amuse and delight thy people know how,
No city presents more attractions than thou,
  With them thou art constantly rife.

Thy Palaces, num'rous, magnificent, grand,
  Are fraught with historical fame;
And everywhere statues and monuments stand,
So pleasing —attention from all they command—
  In memory of some honoured name.

The dome of the Invalides glittering is seen,
  Where Napoleon I. lies interred
In a tomb of red marble, dazzling with sheen;
And who more successful in warfare has been?
  And who of his wars have not heard?

O Paris! thy wonders can never be told,
  Nor treasures be fully explored;
The fruits of both science and art they unfold,
In paintings, in sculpture, in silver, and gold,
  And with them thy buildings are stored.

Most beauteous and bright thy surroundings appear,
  Within Papal darkness is found;
But from superstition deliverance is near,
For lo! now the Gospel is shining quite clear,—
  And will shine in thy midst all around.

King Christmas.

King Christmas is here,
  With jolly good cheer,
Scattering his favours around;
  Quaint carols are sung,
  And the bells are rung,
And all hearts with gladness abound.

These sweet Christmas chimes,
  Remind us of times,
When distant friends lovingly meet,
  To talk o'er the past,
  While the wintry blast,
Is furiously driving the sleet.

The mistletoe bough,
Has attractions now
Which Christmas alone can inspire;
The holly so green,
Is everywhere seen,
And the great yule-log on the fire.

The ingle is bright,
And all hearts are light;
The tables are laden with cheer;
Enigmas pass round,
And pastimes abound,
For merry old Christmas is here.

Draw, draw round the fire,
Let peans rise higher
In praise of the hoary old King;
He tells of the morn,
When Jesus was born,
To save us,—and happiness bring.

How angels were heard,
And shepherds were stirr'd
To seek for the heavenly stranger;
How glory shone round,
And Jesus was found
In Bethlehem laid in a manger.

Then welcome old King,
Thy praises we'll sing,
To thee our hearts gladly shall bow;
Thy tidings of joy,
Our tongues shall employ,
No monarch more welcome than thou.

A Tribute of Affection

TO ELIZABETH, THE DAUGHTER OF MR. AND MRS. STOCKDALE,

ON COMPLETING HER FIRST YEAR.

My charming, lovely, little one,
　Thy natal-day is past;
One short revolving year has gone,
　Since I beheld thee last.

I saw thee on the very day,
　When thou first saw the light;
'Twas in the pleasant month of May,
　When all was warm and bright.

The lambs were sporting in the field,
　The bees were humming by,
The birds intent their nests to build,
　And larks were warbling high.

The fields were clad in verdure new,—
　The trees with blossoms fair;
And countless flowers of every hue,
　Perfumed the ambient air.

The music of the rippling brook,
　Fell sweetly on the ear;
And Sol, with pleasure, seem'd to look
　On all,—our hearts to cheer.

'Twas then, thou came, a tiny thing,
Thy parents' love to share ;
Just like an opening bud in Spring,—
Quite beautiful and fair.

Thy brothers welcom'd thee with joy,
And softly kiss'd thy cheek ;
The pleasure thou didst give each boy,
Was more than tongue could speak.

May goodness crown thy future days,
And Jesus be thy guide,
Till thou shalt sing the heavenly lays,
Exalted by His side.

In Memoriam.

A SONNET ON THE SUDDEN DECEASE OF W. S. NAYLER, ESQ.,
LATE OF WEDNESBURY, 1874.

THE tear of sympathy will start,
And sadness press the mind and heart,
For many, many coming days,—
And gloom exclude the brightest rays,
Inflicting still a keener smart.
Ah! yes, some hearts are quite unstrung,
And harps are on the willows hung,
And songs of joy remain unsung,
Because we have been call'd to part
With one, whose kind and genial ways
Shed brightness like the solar blaze ;
But, ah ! look up,—before the throne
He now appears a shining one,
And hears his Master say, " WELL DONE."

VALEDICTORY.

Written on Leaving the Isle of Man, in the Year 1846.

Lovely Mona! fare-thee-well!
I am call'd elsewhere to dwell;
I must quit thy peaceful shore,
Shall I ever see thee more?

I must leave thy lofty hills,—
Rural glens,—and murm'ring rills,—
Shaded walks,—and beaut'ous strand;
I must leave thee,—happy land.

Often I have wander'd o'er
Thy rich meads and sea-girt shore ;
Listen'd to the sea-gull's yell,
But those day are gone,—farewell !

I have seen thy fishermen
Sally forth to sea,—and then
Bring a rich and plent'ous store
Of the finny-tribe to shore.

I have watch'd the ocean's wave,
Thy rude cliffs pacific lave ;
And I've seen it foam and dash,
As if bent thy cliffs to crash.

But those sights I must forsake,
And my leave of all must take ;
Mona's sons, and daughters too,
I must bid you all adieu.

Lovely Mona! fare-thee-well !
Of thy beauties I will tell ;
And when distant 'cross the sea,
I will still remember thee.

Farewell to Wales.

A.D. 1864.

ADIEU ! adieu ! romantic Wales,
Oft I've admired thy verdant vales,
But now to all thy hills and dales,
          I say, farewell !
To distant friends, enchanting tales
          Of thee I'll tell.

I'll speak of mountains tow'ring high,
Cloud-capp'd as though they touch'd the sky,
Where birds of prey are seen to fly,
          And gain the steep
O'er-hanging rocks,—with ravines nigh,
          Both wide and deep.

I'll speak of dashing, foaming streams,
How each with wildest grandeur teems,
And in the sun-light brightly gleams,
          Surmounting rocks ;
At each obstruction angry seems,
          And hoarsely mocks.

I'll speak of mines,— a boundless store
Of peerless, priceless, sparkling ore ;
And of thy undulating shore
        I'll often tell,
Where strangely mingle ocean's roar
        With sea-gull's yell.

I'll speak of forests, where the pine
And wide-spread oak and beech combine,
With poplars, tall—majestic—fine,
        To strike the eye ;
Round which the ivy's tendrils twine,
        And never die.

I'll speak of meadows always green,
Bestrewed with flowers of every mien,
Where herds of cattle may be seen,
        And children play ;
And gardens too enhance the scene,
        All rich and gay.

But most of all, I'll speak of days
When Christians met for prayer and praise,
And made resound with joyful lays,
        Thy hills and dales,
In num'rous fanes which strike the gaze
        All throughout Wales.

Then fare-thee-well, romantic Wales,—
Thy lofty hills and lowly dales,
And hallowed shrines where truth prevails,
        Can I efface
From mem'ry, when in distant vales,
        I find a place ?

Ah ! no, fair *Cambria*, scenes so grand !
Thy picturesque, entrancing land,
With here and there a Christian band,
   Impress my heart,
And draw this tribute from my hand,
   When call'd to part.

Farewell to Macclesfield.

WRITTEN IN THE PUBLIC PARK, IN THE YEAR 1866.

MACCLESFIELD ! I bid thee adieu ;
 From thee I must shortly depart ;
Fresh persons and places anew,
 Now claim my attention and heart :
Though scenes peradventure quite strange
 May open before me e'er long,
I will not forget thee, nor change ;
 'Twould be both ungrateful and wrong.

I'll think of thy suffering ones,
 In indigence pining away,
And pity thy hard-toiling sons
 Who earn a mere pittance each day.
May Commerce o'er thee quickly shed
 Her blessings of plenty and peace,
And lift up each heart and each head,
 Then murm'ring and sorrow will cease,

I'll think of the Christians who meet
    In thy num'rous houses of prayer,
Uniting in harmony sweet,
    And feeding on rich manna there.
With some I have often enjoyed
    The presence and blessing of Heaven ;
And in Jesus' service employed
    The talents to me He hath given.

I often will think of this Park—
    Its fountains, flowers, shrubs, and green-sward,
Where the songs of the linnet and lark,
    Have inspired the muse of the bard :
And here, without any alloy,
    I've seen groups of children at play ;
And boys in a transport of joy,
    Pursuing gymnastics all day.

I stand on the Mount with delight,
    Admiring the scenery around,
(All lovely and picturesque quite,)
    As though I had Paradise found ;
Yon hills in the distance, how grand !
    How charming " White Nancy "* appears !
And there, on the right as I stand,
    The Old Church its lofty head rears.

The Cemetery ground is close by,
    With spiral and beautiful fanes,
All pointing to mansions on high,
    Where Jesus eternally reigns ;
And there is the Grammar School, too,
    Where youths for instruction resort ;
The play-ground is also in view,
    Where they enjoy athletic sport.

---

* A small white house on a hill, just above Bollington,

How num'rous the buildings appear,
  As I from this eminence gaze !
But those to my heart are most dear,
  Where Christians unite in God's praise.
They sing of the glories of heaven,
  And hear of the LAMB on the throne,
Who for our salvation was given,
  And hath our iniquities borne.

This Park is with beauty replete,
  Away from the din of the town,
Affording a welcome retreat,
  When nature with care is bow'd down.
But now, I must bid thee farewell,
  Thy suburbs so beaut'ous and fair ;
And when in the distance I dwell,
  I'll think of thee frequently there.

Adieu to St. Ives, Cornwall, 1862.

FAREWELL, I must say to the friends whom I love,
Adieu, till we meet in yon kingdom above ;
There, there sounds of parting are never once heard,
Nor mem'ry by sad reminiscences stirr'd.

'Tis here we are subject to changes and grief,
And here we shed tears which afford us relief ;
Our partings are painful,—our griefs who can tell ?
Sad, sad are our hearts when we say "friends, farewell"!

Mutation !—thy mark is impress'd on the earth,
And man is thy subject, yes, e'en from his birth ;
Above, and around him, things tell of thy reign,
And pleasure and sorrow are seen in thy train.

In heaven, mutation, can never annoy,
There's pleasure unending, and fulness of joy ;
Communion unbroken with spirits divine,
And with them, in glory, for ever we'll shine.

Towards that better land, let us constantly aim,
Regardless of changes, wealth, pleasure, or fame ;
Though parted in body, our spirits are joined,—
In Christian affection and purpose combined.

On earth, we've had fellowship, frequent and sweet ;
But again, peradventure, we ne'er may meet ;
Yes, in heaven we'll join, and O, who can tell
The bliss that's ne'er marr'd by the sad word,
    FAREWELL !

Farewell to the Old Year.

ADIEU, old friend, thy days are almost gone,
The remnant of thy time is passing on,
    And soon will cease to be ;
But still, in this, thou art not quite alone,
    For others pass with thee.

Thy course, old friend, has been a chequered scene,
Bright spots appearing, with dark shades between,
    Pleasure and pain anon :
Thy visage strangely mutable has been,—
    Pleasing and wobegone.

And now, old friend, thy dying moans are heard,
And many hearts by them are greatly stirr'd,
    Of old as well as young :
Perchance a dirge is sung by some lone bird,
    But our harps are unstrung.

Ding—dong,—there goes, old friend, the solemn bell,
With measured strokes it sounds thy parting knell,
    The last, sad stroke is near ;
And who, thy brief biography will tell,
    And shed for thee a tear ?

Lo ! too, thy winding-sheet, old friend, is spread,
All Nature droops as if thou now wert dead ;
    Boreas wails and moans :
We grieve for thee, and thy last moments dread,
    Speaking in muffled tones.

Farewell ! old friend, we ne'er shall see thee more,
When thou hast quitted once this mundane shore,
    But cannot be forgot :
Another year, as we have seen before,
    Will follow thee I wot.

Hark ! hark ! I hear some merry bells now ringing,
And all around I hear glad voices singing,
    To hail the new-born year :
With this new friend fresh hopes and joys are springing,
    And life renews its whirr.

So let the soul renew its upward flight,
And with the year increase in hope and might,
    To gain eternal day ;
Where faith and hope will be eclipsed by sight,
    And seasons fled away.

Finale.--A Fragment.

Go, little Volume, go,—
   Thy humble mission start ;
To please both high and low,
   And comfort every heart :
In every house, spread wholesome cheer,
And gain in each, a " WELCOME HERE."

LIST OF SUBSCRIBERS.

	No.
Allen, The Venerable Archdeacon, Lichfield	2
Anstice, W., Esq., Madeley	1
Adams, Mr., Shrewsbury	1
Alcock, Miss, Oakengates	1
Atty, Rev. R. B., Priorslee Vicarage	1
Ashley, Mr. S., St. Georges	1
Adey, Mr. W., Oakengates	1
Bickersteth, Very Rev. Dean, Lichfield	2
Brooke, J. T., Esq., Shifnal	2
Belton, Mr. W. H., Wellington	2
Benbow and Davies, Messrs., Wellington	2
Bourne, Mr. T. J., Oakengates	1
Bourne, Mr. John, Oakengates	1
Bourne, Mr. E., Donnington	1
Brown, A. H., Esq., M.P., Liverpool	1
Bingham, Mr. E., Shifnal	1
Burroughs, Mr. J., Ketley	1
Barker, Mr. R., Oakengates	1
Barber, Mrs., Wellington	1
Bowring, Mr., Wellington	1
Bates, Mr. J., Wellington	1
Bidlake, J., Esq., Wellington	1
Bullock, Mr. W., Wellington	1
Butler, Rev. T. L., Christ Church Vicarage, Wellington	1
Barton, Rev. J., Hadley Vicarage	1
Blakemore, Mr. N., Ketley Bank	1
Brookes, Mr. G., Oakengates	1
Bacon, Mr. J., Ketley	1
Belbin, Mr., Shrewsbury	1
Bennett, Mr., St. Georges	1
Bayley, Mr., Wellington College, Wellington	3
Bowen Mrs., Oakengates	1
Bott, Mr. B., Oakengates	1
Blakemore, Mr. J., Oakengates	1
Barron, Mr., Ketley	1
Barrie, Mrs., Wednesbury	1
Bullock, Mr. J. G., Wednesbury	1
Bostock, Mrs., Manchester	1
Britain, Mr., Newport, Salop	1
Bennett, Mr. Henry, Wellington	1
Breeze, Mr., Poynton Grange	1

Callaway, Dr., Wellington 1
Conor, Rev. J. R., Cheltenham 1
Chettle, Rev. W. W., Bradley 1
Cranage, Dr., Wellington 1
Clift, Mr. E. C., Wellington 1
Corbett, Mr. W., Wellington 1
Corbett, Mr. J. W., Wellington 1
Corbett, Mr. R. L., Oakengates 1
Capsey, Mr. E. J., Wellington 1
Corfield, Mr. W., Snedshill 1
Corbett, Mr. J. W. Mannerley Lane 1
Crewe, Rev. J., Oakengates 1
Clarke, Mr. A., Wednesbury 1
Collis, Mr. R., Wellington 1
Cadman, Mrs. E., Mossy Green 1

Deane, Mr., St. Georges 2
Dudley, Mr. E., Oakengates 1
Dixon, Mr. C., Wellington 1
Davies, Rev. J. B., Waters Upton Rectory . . . 1
Daltry, Rev. V. G., Ketley 1

Ellis, A. D., Esq., Priorslee 1
Evans, Mr. W., Liverpool 1
Espley, Mr. W., Wellington 1
Edwards, Mrs., Oakengates 1

France-Hayhurst, H. H., Esq., Wrockwardine Hall . . 2
Fawkes, Rev. T. R. J., Wellington 1
Fox, Mr. E., Ketley Bank 1
Ferriday, Mr. D., Oakengates 1
Ferriday, Mr. A., Oakengates 1
Ferriday, Mr. F., Stirchley 1
Fielden, Mr. J. C., Red Lake 1
Forgham, Mr. J., Ketley Bank 1
Foley, Mrs., Wednesbury 1
Farmer, Mr. J., Stratford-on-Avon 1

Granville, The Right Hon. Earl, London . . . 1
Grimes, Rev. Dr., Stanton-on-Hine Heath Vicarage . . 4
Groom, Mr. R., Wellington 2
Groom, Mr. T., Wellington 2
Groom, Mr. R. A., Wellington 1
Gordon, Rev. Dr., Newport, Salop 1
Goodman, Mr., Oakengates 1
Greene, Messrs., Wellington 2
Griffin, Mr., Priorslee 2
Grace, Rev. A. Z., Wellington Vicarage . . . 1

Griffiths, Mr., Priorslee - - . - - 1
Green, Mr. J., Oakengates - - - - - 1
George, Mr., Oakengates - - - - - - 1

Herbert, Hon. R. C., Orleton Hall, Wellington - - - 1
Hill, Mr. A. E., Wednesbury - - - - - 1
Hobson, Rev. S., Uppington - - - - - 1
Harrington, Mr. J., Bilston - - - - - 1
Hogarth, Mr., Keswick - - - - - 1
Hutchinson, Mr., Apley - - - - - - 1
Hunt, Mr. W., Oakengates - - - - - 1
Howells, Mr. J., Oakengates - - - - - 1
Howells, Mr. A., St. Georges - - - - - 1
Hancox, Mr., Ketley Bank - - - - - 1
Hall, Mr. J., Wellington- - - - - - 1
Heywood, Mr., Wellington - - - - - - 1
Hobson, Mr. H., Wellington - - - - - 1
Horton, Mr. W, Oakengates - - - - - 1
Holmes, Mrs., Oakengates - - - - - 1
Holmes, Mr. J., Shifnal - - - - - 1
Holmes, Mr. H., Ketley Bank - - - - - 1
Hitchen, Mr. T., Wednesbury - - - - 1
Hitchen, Mr. W., Wednesbury - - - - - 1
Hallows, Mr., Red Lake - - - - - 1
Hiatt, Mrs., Wellington - - - - - 1

Icke, Mr. T., Oakengates - - - - - - 1

Judson, Rev. Josephus, Wellington - - , - 2
Jervis, Mr. T., Oakengates - - - - - 1
Johnson, Mr. J. E., Chicago, United States - - - 1
Juckes, Mr., Oakengates - - - - - - 1
Jones, Mr. H., Oakengates - - - - - 1
Jones, Mr. J. S., Snedshill - - - - - 1
Jones, Dr., Oakengates - - - - - 1
Jones, E., Esq., St. Georges - - - - - 1
Jones, Mr. T. W., Wellington - - - - - 1

Knowles, I., Esq., Wellington - - - - - 1
Knight, Mr.,,Ketley Bank - - - - - 1
Kitching, Mr., Oakengates - - - - - 1
Kite, Mrs., Wrockwardine Wood - - - - 1
Kibble, Mr. T., Ketley - - - - - - 1
Kynoch, John, Esq., Wellington - - - - 1

Lewis, Rev. W. D., Shrewsbury - - - - - 1
Leake, J., Esq., Shifnal - - - - - 1
Littlehales, Mr., Wellington - - - - - 1

Lane, Mr. J., Oakengates . . . 1
Lowe, Mr. J., Oakengates 1
Lewis, Mr. W., Oakengates 1
Lee, Mr. D., St. Georges 1
Lawrence, Mr. E., Wellington . . . 1
Leekly, Mrs., Galena, U.S. 1

McLean, J. Howard, Esq., Aston Hall, Shifnal . . 12
Mayer, Dr., Oakengates 1
Mackrory, J. Esq., Little Hales, Newport . . 1
Mansell, Mr. H., Oakengates 1
Moore, Mr. A. H., Oakengates · . . . 1
Moore, Mr. G., Castleton · 1
Merrington, Mrs., Old Park · . . . 1
Morgan, Mr. Oakengates · 1
Morgan, Mr. A., Wellington 1
Maddock, Mr. J., Oakengates . . . 1
Marrion, Mrs., Oakengates 1
Millman, Mr. J. Oakengates 1
Morris, Mr. W., Oakengates . . . 1
McCarthy, Dr., St. Georges 1
Millington, Miss, Ketley · . . . 1
Millington, Mr., Wellington 1

Nayler, Major, Wednesbury . . . 1
Newman, Mr. W., Wellington 1
Newton, Mr. G., Wellington 1

Oake, Rev. R. C., Madeley . 1
Ogden, Mr. R., Manchester . . 1
Owen, Rev. T., Ketley Vicarage . . 1
Owen, Mr. H., Ketley . . . 1
Owen Mrs., Wellington . . . 1

Perrott, W., Esq., Priors Lee Hall . . 4
Partridge, Mr. W., Wellington . . 4
Pritchard, Mr. T., Oakengates . . 1
Palin, Mr. W., Oakengates . . 1
Parker, Mr., Oakengates . . 1
Pearce, Mr. John, Oakengates . 1
Poole, Mr., Oakengates . 1
Pitchford, Mr. E., Red Lake . 1
Pitchford, Mr. H., Ketley Bank 1
Paterson, Mr. T., Wellington . . 1
Paterson, Mr. E., Wellington . 1
Pigott, Mr. E. W. S., Wellington . . 1
Pooler, Mr., Wellington . 1

Price, Mr. P., Ketley Bank . . . 1
Price, Mr. J., Hadley . . . 1
Price, Mr. Jos., Leegomery . . . 1
Price, Mr., Wellington . . 1
Price, Mr., Ketley . . . 1
Payne, Mr. T., Oakengates . . 1
Pointon, Mr., Oakengates . . . 1
Panter, Rev. J. A., St. Georges Vicarage 1
Phillips, Mr. J., Wolverhampton . . 1
Powell, Mr. M., Oakengates . 1

Rees, Rev. J., Dawley . . 1
Rider, Dr., Wellington . . 1
Ross, Mr. T. H., Wellington 1
Roper, Mr. A., Wellington . . . 1
Ruscoe, Mr., Oakengates . . 1
Rushton, Mr. W. H., Oakengates . . 1
Richards, Mr. W. H., Oakengates . 1
Robinson, Mr. R., Wednesbury 1
Rigby, Mr. B., Oakengates . . 1

Snow, Mr., St. Georges . . 1
Sabben, Rev. W. M., Wombridge Vicarage . 1
Stafford, The Most Noble Marquis of, Trentham Hall . 1
Slaney, Mr. J. H., Wellington . . 1
Shepard, Mr. H., Wellington . . . 1
Shaw, Mr., Wellington 1
Stone, Mr., Wellington . . 1
Slaney, Mr. A. Oakengates . 1
Shuker, Mr. W., Oakengates . 1
Skipp, Mr., Oakengates . . 1
Stocks, Mr., Oakengates . . . , 1
Sutton, Miss, Carlisle . . 1
Strutt, Mr. G., Wednesbury . . . 1

Todd, Rev. G., Wrockwardine Wood Rectory . 1
Tuthill, Rev. G., Wednesbury 1
Taylor, W. M., Esq., Wellington . . 1
Tipton, E., Esq., Priors Lee . . . 1
Tucker, Mr., St. Georges . . . 1
Teague, Mr. J., Oakengates 1
Turner, Mr. M., Oakengates . . 1
Tudor, Mr., St. Georges . 1
Trevor, Mr., Hadley . 1

Unsworth, Mr., Wellington . , 1

Vyse, R., Esq., Norwood, London 1
Vaughan, Mr. J., Red Lake . . 1

White, Rev. W. G., Beverley . . 1
White, Miss, Gateshead 1
White, W, Esq., Edinburgh 1
White, Rev. I., Newport, Monmouthshire . 1
White, Mr. I., Wishaw, Scotland . . . 6
White, Mr. E. A., Roslin, Scotland . . 1
Wright, Mrs., Carlisle 1
Wyatt, Mr., Wellington . 1
Watkiss, Mr. A., Oakengates . . . 1
Woodall, Mr. J., Shrewsbury . . . 1
Wilson, Mr, E., Wednesbury . . 1
Weston, Mr. J. H., Wrockwardine Wood . 1

York, Mr. G. H., Wellington . . 1
Yeomans, Mr. A. W., Wellington . . . 1
Yates, Mr., Wednesbury . . . 1

Hobson & Co., Shropshire Printing Works, Wellington.